novum pro

AF009975

CHASING DAYDREAMS

Michelle Round

novum pro

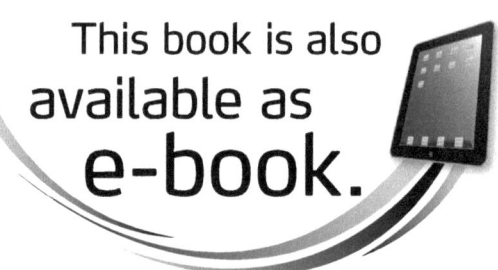

www.novum-publishing.co.uk

All rights of distribution, including film, radio, television, photomechanical reproduction, sound carrier, electronic media and reprint in extracts, are reserved.

Printed in the European Union, using environmentally-friendly, chlorine-free and acid-free paper.

© 2016 novum publishing

ISBN 978-3-99048-202-5
Editor: Nicola Ratcliff
Cover photos: Dmitriy Cherevko, Jeremy Swinborne | Dreamstime.com
Cover design, layout & typesetting: novum publishing

www.novum-publishing.co.uk

Prologue 1

The five foot eight, green eyed beauty stood at the counter in her Father's greengrocer's shop, busying herself by cleaning the counter. It was early February and the weather seemed to be getting colder, penetrating her hands through her fingerless gloves. Despite the crispness of the air, she could see no blue sky, only a heavy grey one that threatened rain. Stretching her over worn, green, knitted cardigan around her she sat down on the small rickety stool and tried to shrink down behind the small, wooden counter. After five minutes her body temperature had started to rise, so she nearly cursed when the rickety wooden door opened and the familiar shopkeeper's bell started to jingle, letting in a waft of cold, wet air. The eighteen year old, who had been voted 'prettiest in the village' for three years running lurched herself up and put on her best fake smile as she met the 'rude' customer's gaze. Then, much to her surprise, the chill that had rippled down her spine only a few moments before, disappeared and she felt un-seasonally warm. The smartly dressed man that stood in front of her had dark brown eyes that matched his full head of chocolate hair and lean features, but only stood a few inches taller than her. Their eyes seemed to be locked on each other and for a moment, the pale skinned brunette forgot where she was, or what she was supposed to be doing. "… Apples please?" was all she caught of the suited man's question as she came back down to earth, "Could I have two pounds of Golden Delicious apples please?" he repeated, obviously frustrated by the dumbstruck girl in front of him. Not wanting to seem rude she weighed out and brown bagged the yellow apples then gave the handsome man his change, watching his every move as he walked back through the second-hand door, this time completely un-affected by the gust of cold air that passed through her.

P 2

The handsome man walked through the small, depressing village of Wordsley with his mother's apples and her words ringing in his ear, "you need to find yourself a woman, someone to cook and clean so you can concentrate on your career." Despite his stubbornness he had to admit, she was right, it was time he settled down. He had just been passed over for a promotion because he wasn't married and therefore considered irresponsible. The girl in the greengrocers had seemed nice, if a little floaty, maybe he should go back and ask her out. She was certainly pretty enough to have on his arm, he could show her the town where he lived. A little country girl like her was bound to be impressed by a busy town, after all he certainly wouldn't be living here.

P 3

By late March the sky was crisp and clear, and the sound of church bells could be heard all through the village. Wordsley's prettiest girl stood in her late mother's bedroom precisely attaching her veil so it covered the bobble that was holding up the wispy bits of hair that normally fell down the side of her face. When she was finished she took a step back to admire herself. Never one for being overly dressy (they had never been able to afford it) she had made a simple wedding dress out of material a friend of her mother's had given her, it was ivory satin with a round neck, thin straps, fitted top and A-line skirt. There were no sparkles or gems, just her mother's old pearls around her neck that still smelt of the perfume she only wore on special occasions. The keen runner smiled at the framed picture of her mother that sat on her sparsely covered dressing table and wondered whether she would class this as a special enough occasion? Stifling tears, she took a deep breath, pulled herself together and went to join her father and two younger sisters downstairs.

Wrapped from the cold by the same shawl her dear mother had worn on her wedding day, and flanked by her family, all in their Sunday best, the striking girl headed out of their small cottage with its thatched roof and climbing pink roses, out through the small white gate and into a quiet, field edged street where only two similar cottages stood. The neighbours that had watched her grow up into the person she was today stood at their gates clapping and wishing her well as she ascended the street before turning the corner that lead to the village church. Once there, her sisters made their way inside giggling like the excited schoolgirls they were, while her younger brother, who was the only usher kissed her on the cheek and followed them in. As the organ began to play, her mother's first born child squeezed her dad's hand and began her slow walk towards her future.

P 4

June 1954

An unhappy woman sat in her bedroom looking at her reflection in the dressing table mirror, surrounded by expensive perfume bottles and piles of designer make-up. The bruises on her chest were getting harder to hide as summer approached; frilly blouses and V-neck tops were out of the question, so she had to resort to round necks with well-placed scarves. The beatings had started when their son had turned one, she hadn't bought the right cake so that night he'd pinned her down on the bed and slapped her chest until she bled. Other times he would go for the legs, punching and slapping them until he got bored, then he would start 'making love' to her, the only way he knew how, hard and forceful until he finished. She wondered what had happened to the man she married, he had promised her a new life where she would feel at home, away from the confinements of the country, a place where she could grow and be herself. Instead she felt like an outsider, watching her own life from the shadows, allowing a cruel bitter man to control her every move.

Night after night she would lay in bed thinking about where it all went wrong, the way he didn't come to the hospital when she went into labour, the fact it took the nurses five attempts to even get hold of him, and the way he only came when he knew it was a boy. From that moment on, he had looked at her differently, suddenly she stopped being his wife and started being nanny, her only job, to protect the boy. She dreamt of how wonderful it would have been to have had a girl, someone she could relate to, someone who would grow up loving her, someone who could have fulfilled her dreams for her.

Chapter 1

The summer of 1975 had started as quietly as any other. I had swapped the routine of going to school with the even more boring task of chores and monotonous trips to the local market with my Mother. I dreamt of walking those grey halls again where at least I had some rest bite from my condescending Father and snappy Mother. My friend Angela thought I was just moaning about my parents, like any other teenager, but she never understood what it felt like to be truly un-wanted. Some days I felt so bored and lonely that I would take any opportunity to leave the house. Going to the paper shop to pay the papers was a treat, it felt like a thrill to go alone. Everytime I turned the corner at the end of my street I felt the urge to start running and never look back, but fear stopped me everytime. I soon realised that the hope of one day doing it was what kept me going all those years.

Four weeks down and my Mother and I were taking the well walked route to Wolverhampton market. A morning of food shopping was the usual numbing experience during which Norma would tempt my seventeen year old self with trendy clothes and accessories only to leave me wanting at the end of every trip. At the start of the summer holidays it had annoyed me, but now I had come to expect nothing so it hurt less. We walked the thirteen minutes into town in relative silence, and then we began at the market. Brightly coloured vegetables and fruits tempted me at every turn, Spanish oranges, and lemons, golden delicious apples and a smorgasbord of British products such as strawberries and raspberries filled the air with a sweet and tempting aroma. This was the highlight of my week, for all of thirty seconds. As usual, my mother ignored the temptations and we headed inside the market, where the only aromas were those coming from the butcher's blocks. Thick slices of chuck steak sat festering in their own blood, and un-lucky chickens sat side by side looking anaemic and soulless. My mother favoured tripe which looked more anaemic than the chickens. I hated it, huge clots of cow's stomach hung over each other piece on top of piece like a mountain of rubbery guts. The worst thing about it was it looked the same when it was cooked. Years later I would be told that we eat with our eyes before we taste with our mouth, by that reasoning I don't know why anyone would ever buy tripe. After a week's worth of tripe had been purchased we exited the market.

    The main shopping centre was only a few minutes' walk away. We were soon in the grey, concrete building, and out from under the humid, overcast sky. The Mander centre was two levels of teenage female heaven. Everything from dark leather handbags, to sleek red flares to white patent stiletto shoes and pastel coloured short brimmed caps were lining the walkways, protected behind floor to ceiling windows. I stared intently through the windows, dreaming of how I would feel dressed up like one of the glamorous mannequins. Despite my thoughts, I would not think about it any longer, I did not want my mother to see me daydreaming, not after last time. Ten minutes later we were leaving the haberdashery area of Beatties department store, with more ribbons and buttons so that my Sunday church dress could be re-invented (again!). It was just then, that I nearly tripped over as I walked directly into a firm chest right in my eye line. After I'd pulled myself together, I looked up, only to see the most beautiful man I'd ever seen. His eyes were brown with flecks of gold, and even in the murky weather of Wolverhampton, his blonde hair was shining. As his eyes met mine, I opened my mouth to say 'sorry' but instead I ended up making a hissing sound that lasted a lot longer than necessary. Clearly quite puzzled by the petite, dark haired girl hissing at him, Mr Beautiful shot me a curious look, backed away and sidled his 6 foot self around me. I watched, dazed as the man of my dreams walked up the concrete steps into Beatties. Unfortunately I was still staring at him when he glanced back at me, so I diverted my gaze and was now looking longingly at the revolving doors. STUPID! STUPID! STUPID! My mother was already halfway down the street when

I caught back up with her. "Are you done?" she asked in her condescending tone, I nodded and we continued the rest of the journey home in silence.

Back home I passed through our hallway with its green mat, dingy flock wallpaper and ancient sideboard that had been my Grandmother's, into the kitchen at the end. It had mustard yellow walls, and new Formica units. The tiled splashback was patterned with the scenes out of a kaleidoscope and was the envy of all mother's friends. I was unpacking the groceries when my mother walked in behind me "You may go to your room now Louise, I will call you when it's time to eat." I did as I was told. To be honest, I didn't mind today, I wanted to spend a few carefree hours in a daydream.

I had the smallest bedroom in the house, right at the back overlooking the garden. The wallpaper was brown with dusky pink roses, and I had the dusky pink shag pile to match. All the furniture was circa 1935 and was the courtesy of my late grandmother. The only luxury we had in this house was that it was completely decorated every half decade. This year, 1975 was the year it all changed, hence the Formica and dusky pink. My mother liked us to be the family everyone talked about, for all the right reasons of course. I lay down on my dusky pink bedspread, I reached for the diary of Norma's late mother that I had found hidden at the back of my wardrobe earlier in the summer.

September 1st 1932
Dear diary,
Again this morning I awoke to the sound of blue jays singing from their treetop hideaways, a sound so clear that I thought they were right outside my window instead of one thousand yards away in the forest that edged Marlborough. I love waking in the tranquillity of the country, but there are only a few more days left before we must return to Birmingham. I can't believe that two months has gone so quickly, I can still remember arriving on July 1st. As we pulled up the long winding driveway, pink dahlias and blue hydrangeas peaked out from behind large conifer trees, and the scent of freshly mown grass filled the air, as our driver pulled the car to a

stop outside Father's imposing summer residence. I wish that I could relive the last eight weeks over and over again so that I would never have to return to cold, damp Birmingham but Mother says it is time we went home and dealt with the business of my wedding.

The man I am apparently betrothed to, visited today and I had to show him around the grounds, all five foot four of him. I still can't believe how ugly he is, I hate his ginger hair and glasses, but nothing is worse than his personality, he clicks at you when he wants you to be quiet, (right in your face normally) and he spits when he talks! How can I be expected to marry this man? He makes my skin crawl! I would much rather marry a man of my own choosing, not the one who owns the biggest estate. Goodnight

As I read on and listened to the finally falling rain, my heavy eyes began to close and I pictured Mr Beautiful, standing in the long garden looking up at my window. Warm heavy raindrops were sleeking through his shining hair, down his face, finally resting on his firm, broad shoulders. Mr Beautiful's black t-shirt glistened in the haze and squinting sunlight, revealing his beautifully sculptured body underneath. Then suddenly I was opposite him, warm rain dripping from my eyelashes as I looked into his golden eyes as he swept me up into his muscled arms, and pressed me against his broad chest. I imagined his heart beating through his chest and vibrating through my head, moving me up and down to his rhythm. As my eyes slowly opened, I could still picture the scene in my mind's eye, but soon reality started to emerge all around me. Almost immediately, my head started to throb, and suddenly I felt the familiar claustrophobia all over again. My body began to feel hot and uncomfortable as I repressed the feeling of 'flight' that vibrated through me. I closed my eyes again but I couldn't clear my head of his image. The more I tried, the more I shook, pressure built up inside me as if I was a balloon about to pop. My back arched and my feet dug into the small single bed as I tried to empty my mind of all this confusion.

"BANG BANG BANG!" I heard the noise and my head jumped off the pillow. "Louise, tea" my brother Phillip shouted at my bedroom door. I was out of breath as I answered him but I knew he was already gone. I felt my back go cold from sweat as I sat up on my bed. Still dazed, I struggled to my feet and limped to the door. I felt drunk as I steadied myself down the stairs and into the hallway. I was thankful that the door to the dining room was closed, as it gave me a minute to compose myself before I had to face the three people on the other side. It was times like this, I felt the flock wallpaper oddly comforting.

Chapter 2

My mother, father and brother were all gathered around the dark oak dining table in the deep red dining room. I sheepishly walked in, my father turned to me and pointed to the seat next to mother (the furthest from the head of the table) and I sat down quietly. Dinner was the time of day my father Michael, the owner of a car dealership enlightened us on the day's business transactions. He did so with his usual vigour that made any error of judgement appear someone else's fault, never his own. Today he regaled us with a ridiculous story about a young couple who wanted to buy a new car. He informed us that they wanted to buy a new convertible MGB, however they were advised against it, because my father wanted to sell them a family car, more appropriate (he said) if they had a son one day. My father's view was that sports cars were for accomplished, single men who had earned the right to enjoy their lives, not young married couples who should be concentrating on building a home and family life. As whenever my father addresses the family, I nod and smile at the appropriate moments, as I quietly eat my dinner. My mother does the same. After my father has finished speaking, it is the turn of my brother. Phillip always spoke with the same mocking tone in which Michael did; today he talked of how he had taken his lady friend out for the day to Birmingham. They went for lunch and he bought her a new handbag, I couldn't tell you the rest of the story because I drifted off around the time he said 'Sharon had prawn cocktail to start'. He then did what he always did, and in his best mocking tone asked me if I had enjoyed the story; I nodded politely and went back to my anaemic tripe. After dinner had gone by, as un-eventfully as usual, mother and I cleared the plates while father and Phillip discussed my brother's progress at the car dealership. I personally don't know how he could make any progress, as he only worked part time; this was so he could have time to pursue his other interests. The only pleasure

I took in this was that the other people who worked for my father hated him, as he was completely incompetent.

After dinner, Father and Phillip headed to the sitting room at the back of the house. The room was small and square with patio doors leading out onto the garden. My father sat in his favourite chair by the electric fire and beckoned to me for his nightly brandy. This had once been my mother's task but since I had been strong enough to hold the bottle, it had become mine. The tray was already set up on the sideboard with two crystal brandy glasses and the new heavy bottle. I placed the heavy tray down on the small table next to my father and he snatched up his glass. The bottle of Hennessey was cumbersome and difficult to hold, so I steadied it with my other hand. It was as my brother started to taunt me that I lost my balance, "little girl can't handle it, we need a real woman to pour our drinks, not a quivering child!" As Phillip laughed, I failed to steady the bottle and in slow motion, I watched as expensive brandy dropped into my Father's lap. I didn't know what to do, the room had gone eerily silent, even Mother had stopped washing up. Keeping my head down, I rescued what was left of the bottle and placed it on the side. I could feel my father's small green retinas burning through me as if they were acid, he stood up and towered over me but I felt glued to the spot. He was 5 foot 10, broad and was still wearing his full three piece suit. He, as always, was judge, jury and executioner. My silence was not providing any reassurance to my father as he pulled me up by my arm and marched me up to my room. He threw me inside and I stumbled backwards onto my bed, lying there, I looked up and saw my imposing father leering over me, taunting me with silence while he raised his right hand and held it there until he put all his force behind it. The slap to my right cheek came hard and sharp, leaving my limp head hanging down as my father silently exited my room. The burning pain coming from my cheek was making it impossible for me to lift my head up, the feeling was familiar and I knew it would pass in a few minutes. The cool tears streaming down my face were automatic and uncontrollable; but also welcome as they stopped my body from shaking and my face from burning.

Chapter 3

I don't know how long I'd been sleeping when my eyes finally opened, I couldn't remember drifting off and I don't remember dreaming., It was like I'd been in a lifeless coma until I lifted my head off the sweat drenched pillow. My face felt tight from the dried tears, and my eyes were sticky and sore. I think it was the next morning, but it must have been early as the house was in silence and I could see the mist lying over the back lawn, not even the birds were singing yet. I was still in my floral blouse and cord trousers from the day before and they made me feel sticky and itchy. I thought about running a bath but the last thing I wanted was to create a disturbance this morning. I always found that, after an incident like last night I should be a ghost for a few days. Not wanting to leave the comfort of my room I stripped off my disgusting outfit, tucked my naked self under the covers and forced myself back to sleep, hugging the cold wall for comfort.

When I awoke again, my father and brother had left for work, and my mother was out with her sister so I decided I could now leave the security of my room, I threw on my old paisley dressing gown and softly descended the stairs. Everywhere was quiet and clean so I crept around, making sure to not disturb anything. I had become very efficient at being a ghost; it just made my life simpler. I padded into the kitchen, made myself some toast, ate it, cleaned up and went upstairs to run my bath, leaving no evidence of my existence. The avocado bathroom suite, with its olive green and white tiles always felt cold despite the temperature of the water, I lowered myself in and sunk down letting the warm water surround me. My head tilted back and rested on the edge of the bath, almost as if on automatic. As my legs floated carelessly in the clear water, I began to feel the comforting weightlessness I had missed over the last few days. I allowed my heart rate to slow and steady, letting my eyes close, plunging me back into my daydream.

Mr Beautiful was kneeling at the side of the bath, his hands gently passing water over my body. He was half naked, and his skin had a golden glow in the haze of the steamy bathroom. I could feel the warm water caressing my skin, tickling the nape of my neck, down my spine as my back arched and under my buttocks, as they rose off the bottom of the bath. He swirled the water around my small navel, and teased his fingers over my flat stomach as the water playfully danced and shimmered in the twinkling light. My body began to tingle as the water moved around my legs, and I gasped for breath as my body tightened and my heart rate quickened. My body twitched to the beat of the moving water and my heartbeat echoed in my ears as I became a conductor for all the heat coming from the atmosphere. My eyes glazed over as he peered deep into them and all noises became distant and un-audible … I gasped for air again as my body lurched upwards, and tossed in the deep, hot liquid. My hands gripped the side as I lost control of all my senses, my head hitting the bath as my eyes flew open.

Mr Beautiful was gone and I was alone in the cold bathroom as tepid water dripped onto the lino covered floor. My head and body ached in unison and I was cold and tired, yearning desperately to be back in my daydream. I quickly washed my hair and body; lurched myself out of the bath, cleaned up, carried my aching body to bed and curled under the covers.

Chapter 4

Mr Beautiful stood in his mother's kitchen trying to change the tube inside the strip light. He was having a bad day, his boss had made him work over, and now that he had finally come home he had to get his toolbox out again.

By the time he got into the small pink bath, it was 9o'clock and the day had taken its toll. As the bath water went grey from the grease that seeped out of his hands and arms he wondered how he would ever be clean again. Sometimes he felt sorry for the woman he was seeing because he can't have smelt good, or looked good for that matter. Mr Beautiful couldn't remember the last time he had enjoyed a bath, but it didn't help that the pink bucket he was lying in was at least a foot too short. After washing himself the best he could in the tepid water, he rested his heavy head against the bath, and allowed his eyes to close. He had only been resting for a few moments when an unusual image popped into his head, the girl from the steps, what was she doing back in his mind? He had barely even looked at her, but she was pretty, not in a sexy sort of way, but there was definitely something about her. Suddenly realising he was pleased with what he saw, he carried on with his daydream.

Chapter 5

Angela was the closest thing I'd ever had to a best friend. She had always been a hit with the boys at school with her long red hair, even longer legs and curves in all the right places. I don't know whether she felt sorry for me, or if she was genuinely friendly but she was a friend my parents approved of so I didn't care. Over the summer she had invited me to tag along to lots of things like family barbecues and discos, but I'd had to turn her down every time. By the end of the summer, I thought she'd given up asking, until I had a phone call a week before we were due to start back to school. Angela was having a party at her house to celebrate the start of our last year at school. I wanted to go so badly as I needed to get out of the house, but I needed to convince my parents first. I wasn't feeling hopeful as I'd been turned down on so many occasions but I needed to try.

I had barely spoken to anyone since my disobedience the week before so the words didn't come easily, as I asked my father for an evening out. He was sitting in his large, ornate chair with his back to the sliding doors. He didn't even look over his newspaper as I stood in the doorway to the sitting room, waiting to be granted an audience. The room was warm with an electric fire as the focal point surrounded by pink, Japanese patterned wallpaper. Un-usually I moved a foot closer and waited again, this continued until I was practically sitting in his lap, and he pointed to a small, old chair across the room, and motioned me to sit down. I waited for him to lower his paper, and then I returned his piercing eye contact. I was sitting far enough away from him that I had to raise my voice slightly so that he would hear me. This was one of his tactics; he would keep pretending he hadn't heard me, until I eventually gave up, and went back to my room. Not today however, today I was determined. I asked my question and waited silently for a response. He was emotionless as he picked up his newspaper again and turned away from me. I sat there in the uncomfortable silence for what seemed like an eternity, until my mother walked in with a cup of tea, so I took my chance and silently exited.

    I sat on my familiar bedspread feeling confused and agitated. Downstairs I could hear my mom trying to argue my case, but I wanted her to stop. All I wanted was for him to talk to me like a normal person but I knew he never would. That thought alone was making me angrier. He hadn't said yes or no, what was I supposed to do? I wanted to be normal for just one day of the summer, he owes me that. I paced around my room, wishing I could talk to my mother about this, wishing she could just see what was wrong. After what felt like an eternity, my bedroom door slowly opened and my mother quietly walked in.

    "Your father says you can go, but you must be back by nine." She said to the floor as she stood nervously in the doorway.

    "Why couldn't he tell me himself?" I asked her angrily. But she was already halfway out the door. I sat back on my bed and tried to take pleasure from my minor victory, but I knew tonight my mother would pay the price.

Chapter 6

Angela perched nervously on the end of her older brother's bed, while three boys from school passed around a spilf, she had thought they were joking at first, but when she walked in on them rolling up, she knew differently. They had been fun and flirty when she first caught them but now they were starting to see through her 'cool' girl façade, she really didn't want to take a drag, but if she didn't, her life at school would be hell and she really did enjoy being the fun, pretty girl who was always centre of attention.

Twenty minutes later, fun pretty girl was clinging onto her parents' bannister swerving to miss pieces of floating yellow woodchip wallpaper that were coming towards her. All she had to do was get to the bottom and the soft, mustard carpet would steady her feet. Three … two … one and down, her mother's prized new carpet kept its end of the bargain and held her tightly as she pulled herself upright, luckily there was no-one in the hallway, so she stood for a moment and focussed on the telephone that sat on the small hall table, turning her back to avoid the swirling panes of glass that made up the front door. As her mind started to come back into focus, she could hear people happily chatting in the living room while Elton John sang about diamonds, and the drugged up boys muffled laughter coming from the behind the shut door at the top of the landing. The thought of her brother coming back from the army base early and catching three kids smoking weed in his bedroom quickly sobered her up and filled her with guilt, "what have I done?" Angela whispered quietly to herself as she dropped her head and re-joined her party.

As Angela wandered through her mom and dad's front room she didn't feel as comforted as usual, her family weren't taking up the sofa watching TV, instead all the girls from school were monopolising the pink velvet setee, chatting vigorously about the boys that were holed up in the dining room (safely behind sliding doors). Plastic cups had started to build up on the mahogany mantel piece covering the array of family photos that proudly adorned the spaces, including one of her brother in full uniform at his passing out ceremony that took pride of place in the centre. Guilt filled her head once again, so she moved out of the magnolia painted family space and into the dining room (sliding the door shut behind her) where the boys welcomed her with open arms.

Chapter 7

Angela lived on the longest street in the world, one side was large detached houses and the other was small semis. My best friend lived on the small side, but I always thought that meant she had the better view. The party house came into view after we went around the third bend and was just as I remembered it. The 1930's pebble dashed semi still had an immaculate front garden, filled with azaleas and roses. My father pulled up outside the house, I hurried out and before I knew it, he was gone. As I walked through the open front door and stood in the very yellow hallway, I could hear Elton John singing 'Lucy in the Sky with Diamonds' from the record player in the living room and Angela's flirty giggles coming from the dining room. Moving through the house I was given sideways glances from the girls in the once immaculate family room, so I chose to ignore them and carried on towards the place where I knew they ate all their family meals. The dining room and adjacent kitchen were slowly becoming covered with empty beer cans and plastic cups as the boys from our year flocked around the evening's hostess, none of them gave me a second look so after trying in vain to get her attention I left the heart of the home and found a quiet place to sit in the big conservatory that spanned the back of the house. Looking around I thought about what Angela's mom would say if she could see all the teenagers taking over her 'perfect' house. Mrs Jones was very much like my mother, but Mr Jones was not, she would spend all the money he earned on fancy furniture and extensions to the house, just so she could brag to the neighbours, and she would always brag about her son in the army, but would never say anything nice about Angela. I did always envy the relationship Angela had with her father though; he was salt of the earth.

I had thoroughly settled into my observer's position when it happened, I couldn't believe my eyes, he was here, my knight, the focus of my day dreams, Mr Beautiful. I sat motionless and un-blinking for an eternity until he turned and looked at me. I think I managed a slight smile, as he walked towards me, but the closer he got, the more I was perspiring, I must have looked disgusting.

He was wearing dark flared jeans and a brown fitted shirt and looked beautiful again.

"Were you the girl from the other day?" Mr Beautiful asked me.

"On the steps at Beatties?"

After a long, nervous pause, I managed a response

"Yes I am … I, erm, I'm Louise Fraser"

"Do you mind if I sit down?" he asked

"Not at all" I said, not quite believing my luck.

He told me he lived with his mother and he worked at the Goodyear factory on the machines. I was immediately enthralled, he had such an easy manner, and the more he talked, the more relaxed I became. Eventually I began to talk about myself, just simple stuff but it felt good to have someone listen to me. I don't know what I was saying when a woman tapped Mr Beautiful on the shoulder, he turned around and stood to greet her. 'She' was tall, skinny and brunette. 'She' looked like one of the mannequins in the Mander centre. As they stood there 'She' linked her arm into his, but 'She' barely looked at me, we were not introduced but I wasn't bothered. 'She' whispered something into his ear and before I could say anything, they were gone. I watched helplessly as the man of my dreams walked away with his stick insect, only briefly catching his eye as he turned back and shot me an awkward smile.

I couldn't believe what had just happened. He has a girlfriend? We had talked for an hour and he had not mentioned her. Why would he be interested in a girl like me when he could have a woman like her? Suddenly I felt the all too familiar claustrophobia and needed to get out. I passed out of the room as quietly as I had walked in, and made my way to the front door, nobody noticed as I left the house and cried on the pavement for the long hour before my father came.

Chapter 8

One month later, we were all sitting diligently around the large dining room table, when my brother began talking of his girlfriend. Sharon was a well-heeled girl who he'd been dating for around six months. She belonged to a good local family who owned a string of hotels in the Midlands area. Her father was well connected and wealthy, just the kind of addition to the family my father approved of (like we really needed another big-headed chauvinist at the table). My Father had been encouraging the match for a few months now, so it was music to his ears when we were all invited to join them for dinner that Friday evening. I think he'd already started to pick out china patterns. Four days later, my father and brother were stood like soldiers in our dark hallway dressed in navy blue three pieced suits with crisp white shirts and navy ties. My mother was also dashing in a cerise skirt and jacket with matching blouse, so when I arrived downstairs in my Sunday church best, it prompted a spontaneous giggle from my lovely brother. My dress was smock style and came just below my knee. I had never liked the colour, navy blue and the new sailor buttons I'd been made to sew on the bodice made it look even worse. It had one purpose and that was to help me blend into the background.

We arrived at the imposing Park View hotel in my father's dark green Rover P5, and he parked in front of the entrance. As we walked down the long corridor towards the back of the hotel, the walls were decorated in oak panels and ornate coving. Twinkling chandeliers dropped from large ceiling roses and chimed in the drought from the main door, as we followed the burgundy and gold carpet into the main bar area, where father lead us to a large table. All around us, well dressed people sipped at their cocktails as my father beckoned the waiter. As usual I didn't have to think about what I wanted, I was ordered a tap water (heaven forbid I cost him any money) before I could even speak.

I knew the Hughes family as soon as they entered the room. Mr Hughes was larger than my father (at least six foot one) and was wearing a long camel coat draped over his shoulders. Mrs Hughes was wearing a long, sage green satin skirt with a matching floral blouse and a cashmere scarf draped around her slim arms. They seemed to be polar opposites, he was broad and imposing, where she was meek, mild and walking in his shadow. Father and Phillip stood up immediately, as they walked towards us, mother and myself followed. The gentlemen immediately shook hands and we all took our seats. Sharon Hughes was annoyingly attractive. She had her father's height with her mother's soft features. As she walked in, every eye in the bar had been drawn to her, including my brother's. At around five foot eight, she was tall and slender. Her naturally blonde hair was cut to a long bob with a full fringe and perfectly curled under at the ends. She was wearing a navy blue shift dress with loose lace sleeves that skimmed her curves and showed off her legs. I was instantly jealous.

The dining room was as expected, decadent and luxurious. The burgundy carpet from the bar had ended and made way for highly polished parquet flooring. Heavy damask curtains in light gold, framed the large French doors that ran the length of the 40ft room. We were sat in the centre under one of the two crystal chandeliers that hung from the white and gold panelled ceiling. All around us sat everything from young, loved up newlyweds to bickering, middle aged couples.

As I looked across our large table, I couldn't help but think that Phillip looked nervous, it was unlike him, especially when he was the centre of attention, but I put it down to Mr Hughes' presence. We progressed through our meal at the normal rate, and by the end of the main course, the mothers at the table had bonded and my father had almost sold Mr Hughes a car. But despite the jovial atmosphere Phillip still didn't look himself, he had gone a little pale and seemed to be sweating slightly. Something definitely wasn't right, despite my feelings for my older brother, I didn't want him throwing up all over the table, he would never live it down. I breathed a sigh of relief, as I saw him slowly move out of his chair and nervously excuse himself as he left the room. Looking around the table I wondered why no-one else seemed concerned, was I the only one who knew he wasn't right? Surely not? Five minutes later I was let in on the secret that everyone else seemed to know. Phillip had walked back into the restaurant but had not returned to his own seat, he had made his way towards Sharon instead. As he got down on one knee, I felt like the biggest fool at the table. I don't remember what his exact words were, or even hearing her say yes, all I remember is the eruption of applause that came from the rest of the diners in the fully packed restaurant. I watched the colour come back into his face, as he tightly embraced his future bride in front of all their adoring fans. Back to where he was happiest, the centre of everyone's attention.

Chapter 9

Mr Beautiful walked into Crane's department store with one thing on his mind; unfortunately it wasn't the striking brunette at the perfume counter who was giving him come-to-bed-eyes. In the last six weeks, their relationship had become more and more physical. On a Saturday they would meet up in her lunch hour and have sex in every place possible. They had done it up against a tree in West Park, against her locker at work, even in a bathroom at the civic hall, but the most common place was in his car. His pride and joy had not been the same since. Everytime he looked at the back seat, all he could see was her spread-eagled over it. He wasn't proud, in fact he was disgusted. All of his mates had gone into Beatties to 'check her out' and had in turn given him a pat on the back, after all she was stunning. She had big brown eyes, and long tanned legs that she could wrap into a knot around his back, but she was an enigma. After six weeks, all he knew about her was that she had a fetish for being 'on top' and was ticklish inside her thighs. The thing was, he didn't want to know anything about her and that worried him.

He continued to walk towards her trying to avoid eye contact, until he reached the Chanel counter. Holy shit she was hot! Just one more ride before he ended it? No! He shouted inside his head, he couldn't do that to Louise, a girl he genuinely had feelings for, despite only having one conversation with her. He stood just back from the counter and waited until she joined him, she smelt of No. 5 as usual, and she had obviously just freshened up her red lipstick but despite his male urges he had to end it, he had to see where this other thing was going.

Chapter 10

Wedding planning was moving a lot faster than I ever thought possible. The church was booked, the flowers were ordered and the venue paid for, so with three months to go, mother and I were walking through Beatties to buy my outfit. I was standing in a sea of stockings, tights and hold-ups when I felt a tap on my shoulder, I span around and there he was, Mr Beautiful was as lovely as in my dreams but I didn't know how to react, until I looked behind him, and there in all her glory was the stick insect. 'She' was staring down at me with the kind of look I get from my father and I panicked. Turning away from him and my mother, I walked quickly towards the exit, my heart was pounding and I felt ill as I hurried out of the store, steadying myself on the cold concrete skin of the building, I managed a few deep breaths. The whole world was still a blur when I felt something pulling at my arm. Looking up I saw my mother, her face was like thunder and her eyes were like that of a snake about to strike. I turned back to the store as she was pulling me down the road only to see my sweetheart standing on the steps watching. I shook my head as I looked at him and shouted "I'm Sorry!" as I was dragged around the corner and out of view. Back home, I ran straight up to my room and buried my head into the pillow. I knew I wouldn't pay for this until father got home, so after a few minutes of sobbing I reached for my grandmother's diary.

Dear Diary,
My head is in a daze ... today I saw the most beautiful man standing on the side of the street. Despite being dressed appallingly, his blue eyes were practically beckoning me. It was an odd feeling, one I have never experienced before, and one I shall never tell my mother about. He crossed the road and assisted me to the other side. As he touched my hand I felt a genuine spark, is that normal? I let him escort me home but I don't

see how it can go any further, he is not of our class and I know Father would not approve. I am hoping that I am just looking for a distraction from my endless wedding planning, but I can't stop thinking about the handsome stranger.

What would be the proper thing to do? Surely a man that handsome has only one thing on his mind? What a scandal it would be …

Dear Diary,

The wedding is less than two weeks away and I can't stop thinking of the handsome man. I am baffled as to why a man I do not even know the name of, should take up so many of my thoughts. As far as I am concerned, he is a perfect stranger, yet I have found out where he works and I keep finding excuses to walk past the shop his father owns. I am so far gone with thoughts of him that I am struggling to remember what I did today, let alone who I spoke to, except those few stolen minutes outside the furniture shop when he sees me and everything is clear for a while. I have made up impossible scenarios in my head where we have beautiful children and a house in the country. Although I know Father would never allow it, I am starting to wonder why I need my father's approval for everything. Maybe that is why I am so distracted with thoughts of him, the hope of a different life outside these judgemental walls.

Goodnight,

Mary

It was 5:15pm when I heard my father climbing the stairs. I quickly buried the diary back under my mattress and rose to face the immovable statue that stood in front of me.

"Your mother and I have decided that until you have learnt to behave yourself in public you will not be allowed out, except for school and work."

"Work?" I asked surprised, "I don't understand."

"I have found you a job to do after school at the local library. You will finish school and will be there until I pick you up at five thirty."

"It is time you learned to be responsible and that your actions have consequences."

"If you choose to let me down, or bring embarrassment onto this household again you will be sent to live elsewhere."

I was taken aback. Slightly bemused, I sat back down onto my bed and replayed the last few moments. I don't know whether this was a tactic, but if it was, it worked, I barely even noticed his palm coming towards me. My skin began to instantly burn as his large heavy hand swiped just below my eye and across the corner of my lip. The force pushed me backwards until I was bent in half with my un-affected cheek lying heavily on the soft bedspread. I don't know what he said as he left my room, I just felt the vibration of the door slamming shut as it rattled through my limp torso. Only when I heard him arrive downstairs did my silent tears start falling.

Chapter 11

I stood outside Wolverhampton Central Library and took a deep breath, the gothic brick structure stood leering over passers-by on the corner it inhabited; a huge wooden door separated the academics inside from the noisy, dirty streets outside. As I nervously exhaled, I pushed all my weight against the heavy door and walked inside. Rows and rows of books encased in huge walnut cases stood to attention around the main space. On the gallery they stood in an arc and nearly touched the ceiling. The décor was plain but it didn't matter as brightly coloured jackets encased every book, drawing my eyes in every direction.

Christine the librarian was small yet buxom, with eyes so small I couldn't decipher a colour, and badly curled, greying hair that she had tried to tame into a small bobble. She made me feel so attractive. She spoke with an authoritative tone and explained that I was to use the trolley to collect books left on tables and take them back to the correct shelf. When the induction was over, she handed me the rickety wooden trolley and I watched her waddle back to the office, her over-sized paisley skirt catching on her loafers as she walked. I couldn't help but giggle.

I took the trolley and started on my rounds, eager to make a good impression. The job seemed a little tedious as I wasn't that into books, the only ones I'd ever read were on the school syllabus and had been too over analysed to spark any further imagination. My first shift passed without incident and at five thirty I parked my trolley into an oversized store cupboard and went to greet my Father.

As my first month of work progressed, I had become more efficient at what was my only task. I had learnt that at around 5pm every day the library became empty, this proved useful as I normally had half an hour to kill before father came so I had taken to reading a book for these last precious minutes. I had decided to take the risk somewhere around the start of my second week. Nobody ever spoke to me when I started or finished so I concluded that they didn't know I was there, or didn't care. The first time I took a copy of Little Women and sat in a concealed corner of the gallery where I wouldn't be easily seen, and began to read. This continued and I found myself looking forward to it every day. This spot for half an hour a day, five days a week was mine, and I could lose myself in the lives of Meg, Jo, Beth and Amy March while my ignorant father thought I was being a model citizen. It felt good to be defying him, and getting away with it, I was even getting paid. The trick at home was to not give anything away, so I was careful to not to show any emotion when father came to collect me. I would get into the back of the car and stay silent until we reached home. I loved the thought that father assumed he was punishing me when he was actually making my day.

I was helping my mother put sugared almonds into delicate lace bags one Saturday evening when there was an unexpected knock at the front door. I thought no more of it until I was called into the hallway.

"Phillip … what is it?" I asked

"This man says he needs to speak with you." He said as he stepped aside, and walked back into the dining room.

My heart literally missed a beat when I saw Mr Beautiful standing there.

"Hello Louise" he said

A stuttery hello was all I managed back, leaving hundreds of questions floating in the silence between us. Just as I began to relax, panic shuddered through my body.

"How do you know where I live?"

"Why are you here?"

"You can't be here"

I stopped and explained when I realised I was verbally attacking him.

"I'm sorry, but you don't understand … my father may walk up the drive any minute"

While I paused to take a much needed breath he jumped in.

"I needed to see you; I can't stop thinking about you"

"But you have a girlfriend" I snapped back.

"Not anymore, I dumped her … I dumped her for you!"

I couldn't process the information that was being thrown at me, so I panicked.

"Why? You don't know me, you need to get me out of your head, I'm not good enough for you."

I could tell he wasn't right, his breathing was frantic and his words were rushed and panicked. He had not broken eye contact with me since I appeared in the doorway and he was shaking from the February chill and adrenaline.

"You need to go home." I said, but deep down I didn't want him to.

"When can I see you again? "He asked, as he started to back away from my door.

I wracked my brain for what to say until I walked up to him and whispered:

"Come to the central library at 5 on Monday, I work there, we may be able to talk a little."

"I'll be there" he said with a sigh of relief.

"Thank you Louise" he said, as he brushed my hand and began to walk away.

I smiled as I watched him get into his old red Ford Capri that was parked just down the road and I watched longingly as he drove away.

WHAT JUST HAPPENED? Did I dream it? I steadied myself against the hall table, and waited until I came back down to earth. It was then that I caught a glimpse of my brother in the hall mirror. He was lurking around the entrance to the dining room, as soon as I caught his stare he began moving towards me. "This is going to be good" he said, smirking. "It was nothing, just a friend from school" I responded. He was staring me down in his most intimidating manner; I started to back away when he grabbed my wrist and pulled me into him. "We both know it was more than that, and if you don't want me to tell dad, you will make sure it doesn't continue, there will only be one happy ending in this family." When he finally let go of my wrist, I backed away and stumbled against the side board again, adrenaline pumping through my body, and tears starting to well up, I needed to calm down, father would surely be home soon and I had enough to deal with. I closed my eyes and took a few deep breaths then re-joined my mother in the kitchen.

"Who was that?" she asked, not looking up from the pink ribbon she was tying into a small bow.

"Just a friend from school" I told her, "he knew I lived around here and wanted to say hello."

She briefly looked up, but I had already busied myself with almonds so she let it go.

My heart was still beating out of my chest. Thank goodness for the loose blouse I was wearing.

Un-surprisingly I didn't sleep well. My mind kept replaying my impromptu meeting between myself and Mr Beautiful. By 4am I had given up on sleep, but somehow my mind was clearer. Like I'd just gone over an emotional wall, and the grass was definitely greener. I realised that despite all my efforts to block him out of my head, he would not leave. Then a thought entered my head, 'is this what love felt like?'

Chapter 12

School on Monday felt like it would never end, in every lesson I watched the clock from beginning to end, willing it to tick faster … then slower … faster … then slower. I wanted the day to end but at the same time I was nervous about meeting Mr Beautiful. By the time the familiar bell rang, I felt glued to my seat, unable to move. The Biology classroom suddenly became a comforting place where I could avoid the big world outside, rather than the stuffy, boring room that made me panic everytime I was asked a question. As I walked out through the protective bubble that had contained me all day, I could feel a lump begin to gather in my throat, the closer I got to the waiting bus nerves I had been containing all day, started to get the better of me and I could feel my hands start to shake. 'Pull yourself together' I thought as I boarded the rickety old bus and took my usual seat towards the front.

The closer the bus got, the more I considered not getting off, maybe I could just go home, fake a cold and spend the rest of the day watching the walls from the comfort of my bed. No! I had to do this, I would never forgive myself if I didn't. The single decker bus that had once been gleaming red but now resembled a dirty burgundy pulled to a stop and I reluctantly stepped down to the un-even pavement, right in front of the gothic building that had scared me for completely different reasons a few weeks before.

Chapter 13

Mr Beautiful slammed on the brakes of his highly polished Capri. He had really put the new Goodyear tyres he'd just fitted to the test. The brood of mother hens crossing the road were glaring at him, just another irresponsible young male, littering the roads. But today they were wrong, there was another reason he had nearly missed the red light, his mind was somewhere else. He had been driving around for half an hour, just killing time until he could see her again. He had passed the library three times, each time his next lap got quicker as he got more nervous. He knew she was inside, god only knows how she was feeling, because he was a wreck.

4:55, time to man up. He parked his pride and joy around the corner, took a deep breath and walked the 15 yards to the library. Steadying his hand on the large wooden door as he hauled it open, he felt out of his comfort zone immediately, he wasn't into books; the last thing he read was a Haynes manual. A portly woman at the front desk was glaring at him through her beady eyes so he diverted his gaze and started to search around the maze of bookcases.

I was pacing around the gallery with my trolley when I spotted him. He was on the ground floor looking lost between cookery and biographies. This was it. I abandoned my trolley and walked to the edge of the gallery. I peered over the balcony just as he looked up. He smiled nervously up at me and I returned the gesture, we kept our eyes locked as he climbed the stairs and walked towards me. I started to back away from the balcony and he followed me towards my special place.

I was fidgeting nervously with my hands until he finally broke the ice.

"I'm sorry about the other night" he said "but I didn't know what to do, I have never felt this way before."

"Neither have I" I responded with "But the woman from Beatties …" he stopped me mid-sentence.

"Oh no, she's just, well, it wasn't serious, we just, you know, messed around, a bit."

This agitated me, and I could feel the annoyance building in my voice.

"I don't 'know' actually, are you with her or not?" There was a long pause as I stared at him.

"I broke it off with her; it wasn't fair to her, or you. I know how she made you feel that day you were shopping; it upset me to see you like that. I'm sorry"

His dark brown eyes looked truly apologetic, and I was drawn in by them. I had never had anyone apologise to me before, especially a man, and it knocked me back. I felt my defences melt away into the floor. I was wide open, he could have thrown me over his shoulders and taken me away right now, I wouldn't have argued. Then out of nowhere I erupted like Mount Etna.

"My life is complicated. I have an older brother who is getting married in four weeks, to the girl of his dreams. My only hobby is reading a diary about my grandmother's love life, that nobody knows I have. My mother has been emasculated by my father who is controlling and abusive, and he never speaks to me except to scold me. I am an average student and I do not wear fashionable clothes, hence my beige cords, and frilly blouse. I am a nothing, nobody."

The flood gates were open; I was out of breath as I finished my speech. Then I stood in horror as I recalled what I had said. Mr Beautiful stood, un-blinking and silent, I think his mouth may have been open in a gasp, but by then my eyes were firmly fixed on the ground, as I wished it to swallow me whole.

"I'm so sorry", I muttered to the floor. "I didn't mean to … er … sorry."

"I had no idea. That sounds like hell; I don't know what to say."

He was silent for a moment. Then he surprised me again.

"I didn't get you into trouble the other night did I, with your dad, oh God, I'm so sorry, I didn't know … I, er, oh God …"

"You don't need to apologise, I loved seeing you, and I just couldn't believe that you had found me. I have been thinking about you a lot, you see."

"Really, that's great, I loved seeing you too. I missed you when I left."

I could feel the heat building in the air between us, he had broken downs my walls, and I was completely exposed. A nervous tension was growing in the silence. I wanted to kiss him. I wanted to climb into his arms and stay there. Is this really what love felt like?

I don't know why I looked around at that moment but it was lucky I did. I caught a glance of the clock in the middle of the wall. It was 5:30.

"Oh no, is that the time, I have to go, my father will be outside and I don't' want him to come in."

I started to hurry away, in a nervous panic.

"Wait!" He called after me. "This is my phone number, call me when you can, don't worry how long it takes, I'll wait."

I stopped as he approached me.

"I promise" I said clearly, and then I pecked him on the cheek.

My smile was beaming as I jumped into the car. Wow! I couldn't believe I'd done that.

I walked quickly out of the library and sat in the back of father's car, trying to stop smiling. I had never been that brave in my whole life and it felt liberating; just knowing that the man in the driver's seat had no idea what had just happened filled me with a confidence I had never felt, although it didn't take long for him to ask why I was so happy.

"I was just stopped by a patron, who wondered if I could recommend a book to him."

"I didn't think that was your job Louise?"

"He stopped me as I was leaving; I thought it would be rude to ignore him."

He looked questioningly at me through his rear view mirror, and I innocently smiled back.

After a slight hesitation he responded:

"That is right; it is good to see you listen occasionally."

"I do my best father." I said back. Hoping he hadn't noticed the sarcasm in my voice.

I felt alive for the first time ever. Not only had I got the number of the hottest man in Wolverhampton but I'd beaten my father. I could tell he wasn't pleased, but I didn't care, nothing could bother me!

Mr Beautiful sat in his car staring dead ahead. Did she just kiss me? He thought as he stared into space. He was rarely surprised by people, but he definitely enjoyed the feeling. His body was charged with hormones, everything had happened so fast. The sexual tension between them had been unbelievable; he couldn't remember ever being this turned on, especially by a peck on the cheek. He definitely got the feeling this would not be the end; he had to see her again. He needed to see her again.

Chapter 14

Mr and Mrs Howard Hughes invite you to celebrate the marriage of their daughter Miss Sharon Alice Hughes
To
Mr Phillip Alan Fraser
On Sunday 21st March 1976
Ceremony to take place at 12 pm
St Michael's Church, Wolverhampton
Reception to follow at The Hills Country Club

Sharon Hughes stood in her bedroom staring back at her reflection in the floor length mirror. Her image had changed so much over the last ten years, from fat to thin, to curvy and now back to slim, she barely recognised herself. The nerves from her less attractive days were still present today, the way people used to giggle when she entered a room and the sneering behind her back. She would have given anything to have a small, intimate wedding, the one she had planned so meticulously in her head. Unfortunately that wasn't good enough for the over-the-top Hughes, her father always had to make a spectacle of everything, just so he could be the big man. However, money did have its advantages, she couldn't deny that she loved how she looked in her designer dress, but one hour before her wedding was due to start it was making her feel hemmed in and anxious. She paced her room, opened the window, even turned on the TV to try and calm herself down but nothing was working. The hustle and bustle downstairs that had been keeping her distracted had quietened down to nothing and now she was alone with the nerves she thought didn't exist bubbling up to the surface. Not wanting to sit down, she placed her perfectly manicured fingers onto the window sill and leaned all of her weight onto it. Only now was her lack of bridesmaids worrying her, if she had any close female friends, they would be a great comfort at this moment. Female friends had never been easy to come by for Sharon. During her school years she had been the fat, ugly girl that none of the other girls wanted to associate with. Then during college, she lost a lot of weight and grew boobs so the girls became jealous of her and all the male attention she used to get. Finally, when she started work as her father's secretary, she was only known as the boss's daughter and nobody (male or female) would talk to her. Never before had it bothered her, but now as she stood alone in her bedroom she felt completely isolated.

Chapter 15

I was sitting two rows behind my mother in the church with my Aunt Sybil and Uncle Alan, the original odd couple. Sybil was tall and slim with high cheekbones and a full head of dark brown hair, but Alan was short and slightly podgy with distinctly less hair, but somehow they just worked well together. As I looked around, powder pink roses and Sweet Williams filled the church with a sweet and enticing smell that echoed the start of spring. The row in front of us was made up of my father's family from Devon, some of the hats were so large that I had to peak through them to see the altar. As I looked over, I could see Mrs Hughes dressed in a fitted satin skirt suit in powder pink, topped off with a brown hat with pale pink trim, she looked as elegant as I remembered her. The church was packed with a lot of older guests, and some of Phillip's friends that I recognised. It was a veritable who's who of Midlands 'royalty' and I wondered if the bride and groom knew any of them. This definitely seemed like an opportunity for Mr Hughes to show off, but it didn't feel very intimate.

Phillip Fraser stood at the altar with his back to the congregation, nervously fidgeting with his cufflinks. Mother Nature picked a good day to start spring, he thought as he started sweating through his morning suit. Behind him, he could hear the guests whispering to each other about what the dress would look like, and how warm it was, but hearing all the hushed voices when his back was turned wasn't doing anything for his paranoia. He hadn't eaten breakfast that morning because of the nerves and he hadn't even told his mother how beautiful she looked because he had been so tunnel minded. The four hours since he got up had passed already, and the whole day up until this moment was just a blur, when the organ started and the two hundred strong congregation rose to their feet, Phillip took a deep breath and focused on the minister.

All our eyes were trained on the door as she walked in. Sharon was angelic as she appeared in the doorway, the sun shining behind her like a halo as she began to descent down the aisle. Oohs and ahhs radiated around the church as she floated towards her groom. Her dress was strapless ivory satin, overlaid with delicate rose embossed lace sleeves and it had a slim fitted bodice that was nipped in at her small waist. The skirt was layers of slim fitting fine silk with a small train that highlighted her long, slim legs, but the train was lost under her sheer lace and satin cathedral veil that followed behind. Her blonde hair was half pulled up, but had been allowed to hang down her back, finished with a perfect curl, she looked like an angel. Phillip turned to see his bride as she greeted him at the altar. As he squinted through her delicate veil she beamed at him with a look of pure love and adoration, her eyes glistening in the light beams darting through the church.

As her proud father took his seat, the ceremony began. We all sat and listened as the adoring couple exchanged vows, and we sang traditional hymns as the marriage service progressed. You could feel the emotion in the room as we sat to hear the final part of the blessing. "You may now kiss your bride" the vicar said, to which Phillip lifted her delicate veil and pulled her near to him, kissing her softly on the lips. The congregation applauded as they shared their first kiss as husband and wife.

Chapter 16

By 12:45 we were all gathered outside the church when the happy couple, flanked by the best man and ushers walked out of the main doors. Phillip and Sharon looked enviably happy as they walked through the huge crowd of well-wishers and into their waiting Rolls Royce. By the look on Sharon's face, I don't think she knew there were two hundred people all clamouring for a look at her, she just looked as though she was in her own little world. I envied her so much at that point; I wanted to go where she was.

I was being transported to the reception in my Uncle Alan's trusty Granada. I ducked down in the back as the old car limped its way up the winding drive that led through beautifully manicured gardens up to the main building of the prestigious Hills Country Club. Waiting like soldiers in front of the huge glass doors, were the valets dressed in their black and white uniforms and top hats looking in horror at the rusty car one of them was about to drive. After they had played 'rock, paper, scissors' to decide who got the Granada rather than the Bentley that was behind us, we walked through the huge glass doors and into the vast galleried reception area. A well-informed porter led us past the angular white leather sofas and glass coffee tables that filled the space and down three steps into the long, sun drenched bar area where the rest of Wolverhampton's elite were sipping Kir Royale and nibbling blinis topped with smoked salmon. My uncle passed me an orange juice and we found a quiet place to sit next to the huge windows that looked out over the short trimmed green blanket that covered the surrounding ten acres. We had only been sitting for ten minutes when a man in full morning dress called us up to start the greeting line. Two hundred equally well dressed people then began milling like herds of sheep into the longest conga line I had ever seen. We waited them out and then dutifully joined the queue. After I had kissed my own father, mother, brother and new sister-in-law, I followed my aunt and uncle to our table. We were situated to the left hand side of the top table, in the corner. The room was huge and contained no less than fifteen round tables, plus a top table that held seven. Each table had been decorated in white cloths with tall vases containing large bunches of long stemmed pink roses. The wall of floor to ceiling windows let in rays of light that danced off the silverware and crystal glasses. It did feel truly magical, but still there were too many people for it to feel personal.

We were sat with what was left of my mother's family. Sat directly to my left was Timothy my cousin. He was the only son of my late Uncle Maurice who had died ten years before. I remember mom going to his funeral but nothing had been said about it, and I don't think she had been in contact since. This wasn't unusual; mom's side of the family had been cut out the minute she got married. Despite this, Tim seemed nice, he was in his early twenties, tall and attractive with a shaved head and huge blue eyes that were made even bigger by his wide blue tie. As they served lunch we made no committal small talk until somewhere around my strawberry Pavlova he asked why I wasn't sat at the top table with the rest of my family. I wanted to answer his question but I didn't want to be too honest and say they were embarrassed of me, so I shrugged my shoulders and carried on picking at strawberries.

"Have I hit a nerve?" he said, not letting it go.

"No, I just don't know the answer ..."

"Don't let them cut you out like they have us, Louise. You must try to be strong like your mother should have been."

I sat there stunned, where did that come from?

"I don't think this is appropriate wedding talk, do you?" I replied angrily. "You don't know the situation so don't pretend to."

Thankfully the Master of Ceremonies called for the speeches to start just before he fired another question at me, so I quickly turned my back on him and listened.

Chapter 17

When the speeches had finally finished I turned to see Tim looking at me apologetically "I'm sorry I spoke out of turn, please don't fall out with me, this will be an even longer day for both of us if you do."

I accepted his apology as he was right; he was the only person so far I'd spoken to. Somewhat inevitably we got onto the subject of dating so I plucked up the courage to talk to him about Mr Beautiful. Mr Beautiful and I had been talking on and off for the last month, I always rang him from the payphone that was outside school, and we talked about anything really. I told Tim how I felt a connection to Mr Beautiful but I didn't want to lead him on, because after all I couldn't go out with him. Tim looked at me confused.

"Why can't you date him? You'll be eighteen next month and then nobody can say anything."

I smiled, wishing things were that simple.

"Do you think that my family would approve of me dating anyone?Let alone a labourer at the Goodyear factory."

"It shouldn't matter what they think, you can't let them control you, it's your life. I don't want you to turn out like your mother. All she knows is what your father tells her. She used to be so independent and head strong, and now she is basically a shell of her former self. You don't want that, do you?"

I knew he was right. I could feel his eyes burning into my forehead as I looked down at the table. After a bit of fidgeting with my napkin I finally looked up and met his gaze. He hadn't broken his stare and I couldn't blame him.

"No I don't want to be like that; but it's not that easy."

I know it sounded like rubbish but for some reason, the abuse and the taunting were familiar, and despite me feeling shunned and belittled by my family, they were still … family. The thing that worried me most was that I was scared about living happily ever after.

Come 4pm and the wedding was finally over. We wished the newlyweds good luck and waved them off. It was only when just the three of us returned to our house on Maple Crescent that I realised home would never be the same again. Should I stay and see what the future holds, for better or for worse?

Chapter 18

The day after the wedding was surreal. The house was eerily quiet and it was like nobody knew what to do with themselves. Apparently, it's like this the day after a big event, like coming back to earth with a bang. I took advantage of the calm and had a day locked up in my room. I cuddled up on my bed and retrieved the diary from under my mattress, eager to hear the next twist in my grandmother's tale.

Dear diary,
As I write this I am still warm from his touch, I cannot believe he kissed me! I was taking my daily walk past his shop window when he appeared outside. He was scruffy and dirty but all I could see were his gleaming blue eyes, and thick brown hair. He took my hand and led me away from the bustling street and down a dark alley, I probably should have been scared but I feel so protected by him. He told me that his father had noticed me walking past everyday and he didn't like it, so this would be the last time we saw each other. I couldn't believe what he was saying; I thought my life was the one controlled by my father, not his. I argued until no more words would come out, how could he do this to me? Seeing a glimpse of him everyday was the only thing keeping me going. It was as I started to cry that he took hold of me and kissed me, straight on the lips! At first I wriggled to get away, but the tighter he held me, the less I resisted, until he stopped and pulled away from me. He told me our lives were too different and his father needed him here as he disappeared around the corner. I was left dazed and alone in a damp and dark alleyway; the air around me was filled with noise of machinery and thick with dust and grease. I stumbled myself together and ran home. How could he do this, how could he shatter my dream so quickly? How could he take away the only freedom I had left?
Mary.

As the sun found my small little window and filled my room with a warm glow, I drifted off to sleep, still anxious for my grandmother. Mr Beautiful was sitting at the end of my bed massaging my bare toes. My whole body felt relaxed and my head fell lightly back onto the pillow as warmth filled my body. He kneaded my feet firmer and deeper, lightly brushing my toes with the tips of his fingers sending shockwaves up my calves and between my thighs. My inner thighs were getting hotter and hotter as he caressed my ankles, moving slowly up my lower legs, circling the dimple behind my knees, and up behind my thighs as he gracefully bended my legs. His touch got firmer as he moved around to the inside of my thighs, firmly pumicing my skin with his warm hands. As he moved higher, my skirt started to rise, and he gently eased my knickers down to around my ankles. My back arched and my heels dug into the bed as he began to firmly massage the space between my legs. The firmer he rubbed the louder I groaned, the whole room was in a blur as I felt the pressure build inside me. I was ready to explode as my body temperature continued to rise … hotter … firmer … hotter … firmer … oh god … I'm going to … oh god … ohhhh …

"Louise what's going on in there?"

My father said after he had banged on my door.

Oh gosh what happened? I thought as my body bounced back down onto the small single bed.

"Erm… nothing dad, I'm just erm… cleaning …"

"Do I need to come in Louise? Or are you going to keep the noise down?"

"NO! Dad, I'll be quiet, I promise."

"Good, I don't want to be disturbed again."

I lay on my bed and listened as he made his way back down the stairs. He wasn't the only one who didn't want to be disturbed.

I sat up and tried to take stock of what had just happened. My knickers were round my ankles and my skirt was gathered around my waist. I couldn't understand how I felt. My body was alive with electricity and warmth, while my head was conflicted;

half of it was relaxed and carefree whilst the other half was full of questions. Would I tell Mr Beautiful what I had done? Was I ruined forever? Am I still a virgin? As the quiet panic began to fill my head I closed my eyes and hoped for sleep.

Chapter 19

Mr Beautiful was lying on his bed staring at the ceiling. His bedroom was quite large with a big window across the back overlooking the long, perfectly kept, narrow garden. Today the sun was streaming in through the gleaming panes, and lighting up his blue walls. He knew the wedding had been yesterday, and wondered how Louise had taken it. He pictured her pale pink dress and how pretty she must have looked, he had wanted to be there, but he knew it was impossible. That didn't stop him being angry that they couldn't be together. As the room got warmer his eyes closed and his princess appeared in front of him

Louise was lying on top of him, her light green eyes staring into his un-blinking, her toned legs either side of his with her knees digging into the bed, resting her petite hands either side of his face. She had him completely pinned down. He could feel himself getting more and more turned on when she began to grind up and down on his crotch, moving her soft lips began around his neck and nibbling his ear. Her warm breath was making his body quiver and he couldn't control his hands as they gripped her firm hips and began to move in tandem with her. He wasn't even inside her but he felt so close to this woman. Beads of sweat began to form on his forehead and his breathing became laboured as he took her in his hands and slammed her down onto his bed. He gripped her small waist as she quivered, arching her back. He was in control now and he couldn't wait to have her, he was going to.

Mr Beautiful opened his eyes, he was holding himself firmly, but quickly let go. His trousers were around his ankles and he was gasping for breath. He collapsed all his weight into the bed and felt himself go limp. His whole body was aching for her … he needed her … in his life … in his arms … in his bed.

PART 2

Chapter 20

I had been on a countdown since the wedding. My eighteenth birthday was Tuesday 20th April. I had the whole day planned, Mr Beautiful was coming over in his lunch break, the house would be empty and we could spend some real time together. We were managing to see each other on and off at the library, and share some well-timed phone calls, but we still hadn't had a first date. I couldn't remember ever being this excited. My birthdays normally came and went without much fuss, but this year would be different. My mother had given me the obligatory birthday cards over breakfast that morning as we shared pleasantries but the mood in the house had been odd since my brother had left home. Father had barely spoken to us since Phillip left, he didn't even say thank you anymore when mother gave him his dinner, I think he was lost without his prize boy to talk to. Mother and I hadn't let it bother us, I think my mother even stopped trying to talk to him, I got the distinct impression that she was enjoying his discomfort.

It was later in the morning that I heard a knock on my door.
"Come in …" I said
My mom walked in and presented me with a wrapped parcel.
"Happy Birthday" she said, as she handed me the unexpected present.
"I couldn't let your eighteenth birthday go without getting you something."
"Does dad know?" I said warily.
"He doesn't' have to know, it will be our little secret … like when you were little, and we used to keep secrets. Do you remember?"
"I do remember." I said fondly as she looked lovingly back at me.
"Go on open it, I want to see your face."

I looked up at her as she stood in my bedroom, it had been a long time since I'd seen her this happy, that was a better present than anything. I unwrapped the pink wrapping paper, and then removed the white tissue. I could tell straight away what they were; the dark denim fabric was looking up at me as I lifted them up of the tissue. Denim flares … oh my god!

"These are great mom! I can't believe that you got me these … they are so fashionable … I love them! Thank you, thank you, thank you …"

I jumped up somewhere around the second thank you and gave her a big hug, which she gladly returned. As my mother left the room, I smiled to myself and giggled. Maybe after all the years of heartache this was the new beginning we all needed.

My mom had left for the shops and I was nervously pacing the front room waiting for Mr Beautiful to arrive. Dressed in my new flares and pink blouse I had found in my wardrobe, I ran to the front door as he pulled up to our house. He was smiling broadly as he walked up the drive to meet me, and I was returning the compliment. He was dressed in a black t-shirt, worn jeans and heavy steel toe-capped boots, he looked amazing. Making sure we were safely inside the house until he took me into his arms, I felt all my anxieties melt away as I rested my head on his broad chest, feeling his heart beating through his tight t-shirt. As he slowly pulled away, I saw his eyes look me up and down. "Do you like my new flares?" I asked, "they were a present." "Very nice" he said, "give me a spin …" As I span round I could see him watching me out of the corner of my eye. I came to a stop and he commented on how nice they made my bum look. "That's just cheeky" I said with a giggle.

I took his hand and lead him into the living room at the back of the house and we sat down on the new setee. We made small talk for a few minutes and he said happy birthday to me, then suddenly we were in silence. The tension was beginning to mount like it did in the library, except this time we were alone. I could feel myself getting hotter as he moved into me, our eyes were locked on each other and neither of us could bear it anymore. Our lips came together like two magnets, and we began to kiss, first gently then harder. My mouth started to open and I felt his tongue push inside, natural instincts took over as I opened my mouth wider and soon our tongues were caressing each other. His hands were around my face and he pulled me in closer to him, I was powerless to resist his natural magnetism so I grabbed his shoulders and kneaded his back with my fingers. As we pulled in closer, our bodies were touching and he moved away from my lips and started kissing my cheek and along to my neck making my eyes and head roll backwards until I had no control. I could feel his hands gripping my back as he held me into him, I was completely under his control, and I was loving it. I wrapped my fidgeting legs around his back and he lifted me up, holding me in mid-air as he bent me backwards and kissed my pulsating chest.

I was still mid-air when something made me open my eyes. There he was glaring at me.

My father was standing in the doorway and I could see the veins in his head pulsating. His face was red and his stare was un-blinking. I had seen that stare so many times but never had it scared me so much.

"Stop, stop, stop … put me down, please, now!"

"What's wrong Louise?" Mr Beautiful said, panting and confused.

"My dad's here"

That was all I had to say to make Mr Beautiful spin on his heels, and stop dead in his tracks. I don't think either of us could move as we stood there dazed.

"Get out of my house!" my father bellowed.

Mr Beautiful did not move, he just stared him down.

"Don't make me ask again …"

"I'm not leaving until I have explained." Mr Beautiful said calmly.

"There is nothing you can say to me that's going to make this easier, so cut your losses and leave now, before I call the police."

My father's tone was getting angrier and more threatening the longer we stood there.

"I am in love with your daughter and I am not leaving until I know she is going to be safe."

Looking Mr Beautiful up and down my father rolled his eyes, "People of your kind do not fall in love, they fall in lust. All you want is to have your way with my daughter and leave her, so do not feed me your lies. They will not work on me as they have on my naïve girl. Now leave my house!"

"You can say what you want about my 'kind', but we treat our loved ones with respect, which is more that I can say for you. I'd rather be poor and kind, than wealthy and abusive."

Mr Beautiful was getting more direct with every breath he took.

"How dare you insult me in my own home, there is nothing wrong with keeping your family in line, it builds respect. Something you know nothing about. I can see your mother didn't bring you up to respect your superiors."

My father was in Mr Beautiful's face and screaming at him. Only now could I see the love of my life getting angry.

"My mother is the most respectful person I know, and people like YOU could learn a lot from her."

They were both shouting at each other now.

Mr Beautiful's fists were clenched and could see my father reaching for the glass vase on the coffee table.

"Stop!" I shouted at the top of my voice.

"This is madness; you're going to kill each other!"

I took a deep breath before I spoke:

"I am in love with this man, and I have been for quite a while, I am sorry if I have offended you but that is the truth. He is a good man, and I need you to trust my decision. I am 18 now and I am not going to hide my feelings any longer."

This was enough to send my father completely out of control. In a glimpse he stepped away from Mr Beautiful and was now completely focused on me. I was backing away when he pushed me and I fell hard against the wall, Mr Beautiful tried to catch me but my father moved so quickly he couldn't. I felt a pain in my hip as I fell onto the electric fire, and slid down onto the floor. Everything was in slow motion as looked up to see my father coming towards me with his palm raised, I closed my eyes and waited for the inevitable blow, which to my surprise never came. After a moment, I opened my eyes to see my father on the setee and Mr Beautiful leaning over him. I don't know how he got him there or what he said to him but a few moments later, he came over to me and lifted me up. I felt pain coming from my hip and my head was swimming so I closed my eyes as he held me against his broad chest, and carried me out of the room.

Chapter 21

I must have blacked out because, when I opened my eyes I was lying down in an unfamiliar place. The walls were pale blue and cream with bright lights that dazzled my eyes, the only comfort was a familiar voice somewhere in the distance.

"How are you feeling?"

As I sat up and looked around for clues, I saw him, Mr Beautiful.

"Am I in hospital?" I said, confused.

"I bought you here after we left your house. You blacked out when we got outside the front door."

"So am I alright?" I asked.

"You have a nice big bruise on your hip, but aside from that you're fine. I told the doctor you slipped down the stairs at home so he wouldn't ask any questions."

"Thank you for doing that" I said, still dazed and confused.

"I don't know what I'd do without you."

"Louise we do need to talk about what we are going to do next, you can't go back home again."

"I don't know what you mean, I have to go back. I have nowhere else to go."

"I can't let you go back into that house knowing what your father will do to you. I care too much for you."

"I know what you mean, but I can't leave my mother in the house with that monster. This just isn't the right time."

Thankfully the doctor disturbed the uncomfortable conversation, but Mr Beautiful stayed silent as I was discharged, and we left the hospital.

"Are you going to talk to me? Or am I going to get the silent treatment all the way home?"

After a pensive glance in my direction, he started to speak.

"I don't know how you can be so loyal to a man who today practically knocked you unconscious. I just don't understand."

"I know you think it's mad, but I can't leave my mother there with him. I owe it to her to stay, to protect her."

"I don't know why, she has never protected you, she just let him abuse you. Your loyalties are in the wrong place. Why can't you come with me and I will protect you forever?"

This made me angry, I would always be loyal to my mother, she had brought me up, and she needed me.

"How can you ask me to leave my mother? Would you leave yours? I bet you wouldn't … why can't I be loyal to both of you?"

He didn't answer my questions as he helped me into the car. This time there was a different tension between us. I knew he was disappointed, but I couldn't just abandon my whole life and run away with him. The drive home was quiet and unbearable and even when we pulled up to my house, he sat there silently. I didn't know what to do, he looked lost.

"Why can't you talk to me? I asked quietly.

"I love you more than you know Louise, and it pains me to see you going back into that house. I know you feel you owe your mother something but one pair of jeans can't make up for five years of neglect and abuse. You have to know that I'm on your side, please don't cut me out."

"I love you too, and I know this is hard for you, but please be patient with me. I will leave, but I have to know she is safe first. I won't cut you out, I promise."

I gave him a kiss on the cheek as I got out of the car and I walked the long path up to the red front door. I turned just in time to watch him drive away. This day hadn't turned out the way I had planned. I took a deep breath as I turned the door handle and walked into the familiar hallway.

Once inside I stood in the hallway on the old green mat and looked around the darkness. Should I go upstairs? Or should I go into the back room and face my punishment? It was then that I spotted the suitcases at the foot of the stairs. I looked up and as my eyes adjusted to the darkness I saw my father standing on the landing.

"Just so we're clear Louise, those are your bags. As you quite rightly explained earlier, you are eighteen now and you are making your own decisions. You are no longer associated with this family or this house. You will leave tonight and I do not expect to see you again. Your mother and I are very disappointed in you."

I was speechless as my father evicted and disowned me in one swift motion, but having nothing to say and nowhere else to turn, I picked up all of my worldly goods and made my way back to the front door. As I glanced back, all I could see were the whites of my father's eyes staring at me in the darkness. He was emotionless and un-blinking as he watched his only daughter walk out of his life.

Chapter 22

Mr Beautiful had driven around the block three times until he parked the Capri on a corner and walked in the Dog and Whistle pub at the top of Louise's street. Inside it was filled with a haze of cigarette smoke and the smell of stale beer. He made his way to the bar and sat on one of the rickety old stools. As the haze cleared, he could see the yellow stained walls, and worn red sofas that hugged the walls, it didn't feel at all like his normal local, where all his mates would be right now, it felt like the end of the earth. Men who had long forgotten what it felt like to be sober, hung over sticky tables nursing pints of flat bitter, while they played with their wedding rings as if they were allergic to them. It definitely wasn't a nice place but it suited his mood. He ordered a double Glenfiddich with ice from the un-happy host and slowly sipped it.

The day had really taken its toll. He could understand where Louise was coming from but he knew all her caring would be in vain. When he had spoken to Michael, he had told him he would take her away which had shut him up, he hadn't known she would not go with him. He felt rejected and beaten, how much more could he do for this girl? He questioned whether she was worth it. As his head filled with questions and doubts he sipped the strong whisky and rested his head on the rough wooden bar.

Chapter 23

I stood on the front doorstep with my suitcases; I really didn't have a clue where to go. I had no money, no car, nobody. I knew where Mr Beautiful lived but I couldn't walk there, it was too far and I felt so embarrassed about arguing with him, especially knowing he had been right all along. I decided the only option was to try and get to Phillip's, which was about a mile away so I started my ascent up the street. The first time I realised I was crying was when my cheeks went cold from the tears. I was about to turn the corner at the top of the street when I couldn't contain it anymore. The calm, understated tears were replaced by a loud uncontrollable wail, as I sobbed in the middle of the road. My bags dropped onto the floor and I collapsed onto them, that was where I stayed shivering and alone.

I don't know how long I'd been sitting on my luggage when the haze began to clear; the clearer light startled me and made me look up. My eyes were sore from the tears and my cheeks felt tight and tender. As I adjusted to the light, I saw it, a red Capri sitting a few yards away. I felt a thunder bolt go through me, and it brought me back to life. I heaved up my bags and started walking towards Mr Beautiful's car. I could recognise it anywhere. Even in the dim light it was gleaming. The long bonnet was smooth and he had coloured it the same as the car in Starsky and Hutch. The car was empty but I could see the pub across the road, I was certain he was in there but I couldn't go in, I couldn't face him in there. Instead I sat down on the curb and waited.

After about an hour I saw him walk out of the pub. I stood immediately as he walked towards me, trying to read his face as he got closer.

"Louise? What are you doing here? Are those suitcases?"

"I know I should have listened to you and I'm so sorry ..." as soon as I got home my dad threw me out; I've been sitting here waiting for you to come outside."

"Why didn't you just come in? You must be freezing?"

"I was embarrassed; I couldn't meet you in front of other people ... I really am so, so sorry."

He stood quietly for a moment as his face softened. I didn't know what he was thinking, but he didn't seem angry.

"You can stop apologising Louise, your heart was in the right place. I'm sorry I pushed you."

After a brief pause, he spoke, "would you like to go somewhere? Where we can be alone and talk."

I nodded in agreement and happily climbed into his car.

Chapter 24

Rose stood in her kitchen waiting for the kettle to boil looking out at the familiar view of her neighbour's driveway, thankfully it was too early for them to be up, the last thing she wanted was for the 'talk' to start already. The house was blissfully quiet as she leaned on the worktop of her galley kitchen, picking at her tea and toast. The sleepless night was the third in a row, ever since her son had asked if he could move his girlfriend in. Rose understood the situation and she didn't want the poor girl suffering at home, but letting another woman into her home was tricky. She liked things a certain way, and from what her son had said, she came from money. There certainly wasn't any money here; would she be able to help out? Or would she expect to be waited on? The mist was just clearing over Ann and Derek's ancient Austin Allegro allowing the sun to penetrate her cornflour blue kitchen, when she heard the familiar noise that normally filled her with relief, no such luck today.

Chapter 25

I sat in Mr Beautiful's car on his mother's immaculate front drive. The semi-detached house he shared with Rose looked very well kept, if not a little small surrounded by similar houses that all needed some attention. The shortly mowed front lawn was edged with bright pansies, daisies and daffodils. I had watched Mr Beautiful enter through the gleaming white front door, and he had been inside for about fifteen minutes when he finally emerged.

"Give it ten minutes and we can go in, my mom isn't dressed yet."

We sat there in a nervous silence for the longest ten minutes of my life.

"Are you ready?" he asked me.

"Not really, but we don't have much choice do we?" I said with a slight smile.

"Let's go then" he said as we got out of the car.

As we entered the small house, I was amazed to see how clean it was. The hall was decorated in pale pink that was sparkling lightly in the morning sun and I could see the light blue paint of the kitchen peeking out through the crack in the door. The carpet was red with a deep pile, and felt wonderfully soft even through my shoes. I caught a reflection of myself in the hall mirror that was at the bottom of the stairs. Before we walked to the end of the hall, I quickly ran my fingers through my hair and straightened my clothes. I didn't want to look like I'd just spent the night in her son's car. We walked past the first closed door on the right and entered through the second. The sitting room was small with white walls and an electric fire. The huge window at the back of the room looked over the beautiful back garden and his mom was sitting in an over-sized armchair that was just in front of it.

"Mom, this is Louise" Mr Beautiful said, as his mother turned around.

She looked me up and down as I stood nervously in her back room. As she stood up, I could see she was a small woman, with a curvy figure, but her face was soft and welcoming.

"Nice to meet you Louise, I've heard so much about you. Please sit down and make yourself comfortable. Would you like a cup of tea?"

I was shocked at how pleasant she was. I didn't ever remember my mother and father being that pleasant to me.

As I sipped my tea out of the delicate mug, she asked me how I was feeling. I responded politely and said I was fine, but her face said she knew I was lying. When we had all finished with our tea and the necessary small talk, Rose led me upstairs and showed me my room. Upstairs was small and I was in the box room at the front of the house. Rose's room was next door and Mr Beautiful's was the other side of the landing, next to the bathroom. It contained a small single bed with a beige bedspread and pink throw, there was a single wardrobe and a bedside table that were similar to what I'd had at home squeezed into the corner. It didn't feel like home, but it was better than the street, I sat down on the bed and tried to take in everything, not knowing what to feel, only then did she begin explaining the rules.

Number 1
    You will never enter my son's room during the times that he is there.
Number 2
    You will not have to pay rent, however you will help with all household chores as necessary.
Number 3
    You will not disturb my son when he returns from work, or during the weekend when he is doing jobs around the house.

Number 4
　You will not be allowed to bring back any school friends without prior agreement from me.
Number 5
　You will have no contact with any of the women on the street.
Number 6
　Meals are at 6:30pm every night and you will be in attendance.
Number 7
　If you drink or smoke, STOP.
Number 8
　All of your belongings are to stay in your room, with the exception of school books or materials which may be kept neatly downstairs.
Number 9
　You must never enter my room.
Number 10
　You shall maintain a good state of appearance whenever you are out or present inside the house.

I obediently sat on the bed she had graciously provided me and said I understood, as she left the room I felt un-easy but thankful to her for opening her home to me. I asked Mr Beautiful if he was allowed in my room, and he said yes, but only during the day. He sat on the bed next to me and apologised.

"It was the only way she'd allow you to stay." He said embarrassed. "I promise one day we'll have our own house and you can do whatever you like."

I smiled at the notion of us buying our first home together and looked deep into his golden eyes.

"You don't need to apologise, I am eternally grateful to your mother for allowing me to come here at all. It's going to be hard though, with you being just across the landing."

"Tell me about it" he said, blushing slightly.

Chapter 26

When you live in someone else's house, you tend to sub-consciously walk around on egg shells. Despite how welcome you are made to feel, a part of you knows that you are not supposed to be there. The biggest challenges however, were the strict rules I was bound by, the hardest being the lack of contact Mr Beautiful and I were having, despite living under the same roof. As soon as he returned home, Rose would have him doing jobs around the house and garden, to keep him occupied. I couldn't help but think it was intentional so we wouldn't be tempted to break the rules. I had managed to keep mostly to myself doing homework during the week, and at the weekend I busied myself with washing and ironing, something I had found out early on that Rose detested. It was my attempt to seem appreciative of all she had done for me. The evenings and nights were the worst. After dinner, Mr Beautiful would go up for a bath and that was my cue to go upstairs and do coursework in my room, the temptation was unbearable. I could hear him get undressed and lower his tight body into the warm water. I often found myself staring at the door to my room, hoping it would become transparent. It never did, much to my disappointment. After his bath my boyfriend would walk across the landing to his room. I always heard him pause before he opened his door as if he was feeling exactly as I was, horny! This continued for weeks until one afternoon he came into my room. To say the least, I was surprised to see him there in the doorway, his mother normally kept him so busy during the day that he had no opportunity to come up to my room. Maybe she was slipping?

"Do you mind if I come in?" he said with a smile.

"Of course not, I'm thankful for the distraction" I replied.

"I know we haven't had much time together since you moved in, and I wanted to fix that." He said in his matter-of-fact tone.

"We are going out on Saturday night, my mate Ian's having a party and he's invited us!"

I was so happy I jumped off the bed and straight into his arms. He had been working outside and was sweaty and dirty but I didn't care. Chemistry books and pages of coursework littered the floor as we held onto each other. I had missed his embrace so I took advantage and nuzzled my head into his chest.

"What shall I wear? Is it dressy or casual?" I asked as I pulled away from him "I've not been to a party as someone's date before; I don't want to embarrass you."

He looked at my slightly panicked face and smiled. "Don't worry Louise; you always look great, but just for you I'll find out the dress code."

"Thank you" I replied, "I want to fit in."

We were still enjoying the rare closeness when his mother called out his name.

"I suppose I'd better see what she needs now" Mr Beautiful said to me, rolling his eyes. "Can't wait until Saturday."

Chapter 27

I had been standing in front of the wardrobe in my dressing gown for an hour when my boyfriend shouted through the door. "Come in" I said, making sure I was covered up.

"How are you getting on choosing an outfit? Do you need any help?" the gorgeous man in my doorway asked.

"I think helping me dress is against the rules" I said with a smile.

"Well mom's not here and I don't remember seeing that written down, do you?"

He had a cheeky look on his face that was making him hard to resist. "You're going to get me in trouble; she's already moody enough because we're going out tonight."

"Well if you don't need my help I'll just take this dress back to Beatties then?"

"What dress?" I said, excitedly questioning him.

"Well I don't want to break the rules" his tone was getting cheekier, "I know how much you love to be a good girl."

He slowly moved a Beatties carrier from behind his back, and then playfully hid it again.

"Stop teasing me, what have you got there? Show me, please …"

I could tell how much he was enjoying himself, but eventually he relented. As he handed me the familiar burgundy carrier I excitedly removed its contents. In my hands I was holding a red silk halter neck dress and a shoe box. I placed the box on the bed and carefully handled the silk, holding it against my dressing gown, gazing at my reflection.

"This is beautiful, it must have cost a fortune."

"You're worth it" he said, grinning from ear to ear. "Apparently this is really 'in vogue' at the moment, or so the assistant said. I hope it fits ok."

"It's my size so it will; I can't wait to put it on."

I found a hanger and hung the dress on the wardrobe door. Opening the shoe box I saw the black leather looking back at me. As I lifted them out of the box, I saw they had a T-bar front leading to a side buckle, three inch heel and a covered toe. They were beautiful, and I was speechless.

"Let's see it all on then" Mr Beautiful said, snapping me out of my shock.

"Go downstairs then and I will come down when my hair and make-up matches my dress and shoes."

"Alright then, you tease, I'll get ready and meet you downstairs. Don't be too long though or I might have to come back and help you."

I giggled as he left the room, and then dropped down on to the edge of the bed. Was this real? Had a gorgeous man just bought me an outfit? I pinched my wrist to see if I was dreaming. I wasn't.

An hour later I stood looking in the cheval mirror that stood in the corner of my bedroom. I had pinned the front of my hair up, and left the back long. I wore neutral make-up (it was all I had) and I was wearing the stunning outfit my wonderful boyfriend had bought me. I had never felt this glamorous; it was a good feeling, if slightly nerve-racking.

I had heard Rose get home about thirty minutes before, and I was anxious to see how she reacted to my new look. As I walked down the stairs, I could hear mother and son talking in the kitchen so I stood at the bottom of the stairs and waited until Mr Beautiful turned and noticed me. It didn't take long and he looked at me in complete awe. Walking towards me, he took my hand and kissed it. "You look beautiful" he simply said. It was enough for me. I was already on cloud nine.

"How do you like the outfit I bought her mom?" he proudly asked.

"It looks expensive; I hope she wears it again."

That was all she had to say, but it didn't bother me; nothing could bother me right now.

Chapter 28

Ian stood in his late parents' house wondering what his Mom would make of the people who were currently getting drunk in her front room. At only twenty two he'd already had a rough few years. His mom and dad had died in a car crash eighteen months ago and he was finding it hard to adjust. Thankfully, they'd paid off their mortgage so at least he didn't owe the bank, but suddenly being the owner of a four bedroom detached house was more than he was ready for. The only silver lining was his best friend (who had just walked in with his new girlfriend). He was the only one who had been able to help during the last year and a half; he was the only person who could truly understand what he was feeling.

As we walked into Ian's huge house, it was unlike anything I'd ever experienced before. Cigarette smoke crept into the spacious hallway from what looked like the dining room on the left, and the dulcet tones of Pink Floyd's Dark Side of the Moon album droned from the living room on the right. We carried on through the haze and down the brown, yellow and green striped hall to the back of the house, past the dark stained staircase that carried the noises of couples arguing upstairs. The kitchen was huge but dated with blue and white melamine units with teak trim, standing on white and grey spotted lino; I could picture my mother rolling her eyes at the outdated style. At the very end of the can littered kitchen sat a picnic style table. As we made our way towards the heavy oak table, my date got a round of whoops and sarcastic claps as we made our way towards them. "Glad you could make it Sir" they said as we joined them. There must have been ten people at the end of the kitchen, all men. My date was holding my hand, as he introduced me to them.

Ian was tall and slim with dark blonde hair and blue eyes. He seemed happy to see Mr Beautiful, and seemed to relax instantly in his presence.

"Come and sit down Louise, and let that lazy man get you a drink." A long haired, scruffy man sitting in the middle of the table said to Mr Beautiful.

"We've heard a lot about you, our boy is well and truly smitten." The slightly drunk, scruffy man began to tell me. "How are you finding living with his mother? Have you had any bitch fights yet?"

"Steve" my boyfriend butted in. "Don't scare her away already, we've only been here five minutes.

"Sorry" Scruffy Steve said, "I've forgotten how to act around a proper lady. The one's I've had weren't ladies at all, if you know what I mean?"

At that point my gallant date pulled me away.

"Right Steve you've had your chance, no more talking to my missus. Come on honey lets go outside."

I gladly took his hand as he led us through the magnolia and brown living room, outside into a lovely garden.

"I'm sorry about him, I didn't realise he would be here. The rest of the lads are alright but he can get a bit, overpowering sometimes."

I smiled and told him not to apologise. "I'm sure he's harmless really." I said, not quite believing it myself. Mr Beautiful laughed and put his arm around me. We were sitting on a rickety garden swing bed looking out onto the perfectly manicured lawn. I turned to look at his gorgeous face in the moonlight and he returned the compliment. "You really are beautiful" he said, as he pulled my face closer so I could kiss him. This time there was no fear, no-one to walk in on us, just me and him in the twilight.

We kissed for most of the night, with the rickety old chair creaking more and more everytime we moved closer together. By the time we came up for air it was 1am, my dress was ruffled and I had red marks on my chest where he had been kissing me. I was ready for him to take me when a drunken rabble falling out of the patio door disturbed us. Men and women in their early twenties fell over the immaculate garden, squashing marigolds and pansies in their wake, we took this as our cue to leave, and made our way through the beer smelling living room. Boyfriends and girlfriends were passionately kissing in every dark corner, the couples upstairs were still arguing, and the poker tournament in the kitchen was drawing to a heated close. Mr Beautiful said a quick goodbye to his best friend and we made a quick exit, almost running to his shiny Capri so we could carry on where we left off. As we pulled up to the house, the tension between us was almost unbearable, he turned the engine off and I jumped out of my seat to kiss him. I was straddling him inside the car, and my nails were digging into his back as he un-did my halter neck. The delicate silk straps straps fell down to my waist revealing my white strapless bra, which he smoothly un-hooked. My virginal bra was lying over the gear stick as he began lightly biting my erect nipples while his fingers danced around my small navel like raindrops, as my stomach tensed tighter. We didn't care anymore, I wanted him and he wanted me. I undid the buttons on his pale pink shirt to expose his golden chest and ran my finger nails down his abdominals towards his heavy-set belt buckle. I could feel his stomach tensing like mine as I dug in deeper.

This time he was the one to stop. "Oh shit! She's awake. Louise we need to stop, my mom's just turned the landing light on, and she's coming downstairs. You need to get off."

He lifted me off him and I sat breathless and topless on the passenger seat. "Louise! Top!" he snapped. I quickly put my clothes back on and composed myself. We waited a minute before we made our way into the house. His mom was warming hot milk as we walked into the kitchen to get a glass of water.

"You're late tonight. Good party?"

"Yeah it was good actually, I introduced Louise to everyone."

"Good, good" she said, "I think it's time for bed though, don't you?"

We both nodded and she went ahead of us up the stairs. As we climbed the wooden hill, I felt Mr Beautiful's hand creep up my dress and inside my thigh, I clung onto the bannister to avoid falling up the stairs and into his mother. I shot him back a glare, but all I was met with was his cheeky smile. He could win me over so easily. I staggered into the room and fell onto the bed. Damn these rules! I thought as I lay there still warm and electrified from his touch.

PART 3

Chapter 29

Norma Fraser was sitting in her kitchen cradling a cup of tea. She had been putting off cleaning her daughter's bedroom for the three long weeks since Michael had disowned her, but everytime she tried to open the door to her room, she felt sick to her stomach. How could she have let this happen? How could she let her own husband disown her only daughter? She couldn't understand how the man she loved so much could be so heartless; how could she turn her back on the daughter she had wanted for so long?

Norma stood at the top of the stairs and swallowed down the vomit she felt rising up her throat, this had to be done; she closed her eyes and bit her lip as the gold handle turned in her trembling palm, only opening her eyes when she was safely inside, with the door closed firmly behind her. The cold hit her immediately, despite it being May, her daughter's old bedroom felt chilly. When Michael had ordered her to clean out Louise's things, he'd turned off the radiator and drawn the curtains. The door had been shut since that afternoon. Pushing her feelings to the side and stifling the tears that were trying to well up inside, she began stripping off the bed, trembling more with every pull of a sheet. Images of her tucking Louise in every night, how she always wanted three covers on top of her whatever the weather came flooding through her mind, but like she had done so many times before, she stayed as emotionless as she could. It was only when she was struggling to pull the fitted sheet loose that she spotted something wedged between the mattress and the frame. Reaching down she pulled out what looked like an old diary, the leather binding was dark and scuffed, and the pages inside felt thin and delicate. What was this, and why did Louise feel the need to hide it from her? Intrigued she began delicately turning the thin paper until she reached the small bookmark about halfway through; she perched on her daughter's old bed and began to read.

Dear Diary,

The weather has been bleak for seven days now, the sky threatens rain, but no rain falls, yet the clouds refuse to disappear. I have been in my room staring at my wedding dress for a whole day but I still do not like it, how is it that a woman can hate the sight of her own wedding dress? Why do I feel that I am making the wrong decision, when my head tells me it is the right one? I feel like I am living a lie, I do not want to marry this man, and the thought of lying to him in God's house is making me feel ill. How would I ever be forgiven if I continue to lie, and deceive those closest to me? With only twenty four hours to go I am panicking, maybe it's just pre-wedding jitters?

Dear Diary,

The sky has still not cleared; in fact the clouds have got heavier and blacker. December is not a good month for wedding, things like this should be done in the spring or summer when there is hope and happiness in the air, not the winter when it is dark and depressing and the streets are grey and frozen. As I write in you, for what I have come to accept might be the final time, I am failing to stop the tears that are dripping down my face, each one splashing onto the heavy paper like a raindrop hitting an umbrella. Today I will be married at 12 noon, to a man that does not love me, or care for me but who has chosen me based on my inherited good looks and inherited wealth. I have come to accept that I am neither happy nor sad, just indifferent, as I have no need for emotions on the path that I am headed. Carefree summers filled with carelessly spent hours walking through the forest, dreaming of the fairies and goblins that inhabit them are gone, and are to be replaced with the management of 'downstairs' staff and gala balls, each one the same as the next, while my 'husband' continues to live the same life he always has, but with the added bonus of an inevitable heir to carry on his estate and a pretty wife on his arm. I am sorry for the future I didn't get to tell you about, but thank you for keeping my secrets,
Sincerely, the future Lady Mary Sandringham (nee Marlborough)

My horse drawn carriage was at the front door, my dress was on and my veil in place while I stood with my father in the foyer of his inherited family home. I could feel my heart beating out of my chest as we walked closer to it. The rain that had been threatening for a whole week was now making its grand entrance as I would soon be making mine. My father stood emotionless as he walked me towards my destiny that he had planned since the moment I was born, not a word about my dress or even a flicker of pride in his eyes as I boarded the carriage.

We had travelled the bumpy mile to the cathedral in silence, as the pit in my stomach began to widen. All around us the heavens opened letting through a gust of powerful wind and lashings of rain, causing people wrapped up from the chilly weather to run into nearby shops and take cover under canopies. It was as if God knew what I was about to do and was punishing me for it. We sat in the carriage for a few long moments while the storm from the heavens passed, making way for the storm building inside me. I could feel the long sleeves of my silk dress tightening around my arms and the supposedly smooth fabric beginning to irritate my neck, I needed to get out into the air but protocol had to be followed and they were not ready for me yet. I looked around the carriage needing to see something comforting but nothing was there, then I looked outside, the grey skies were heavy and oppressive and threatened us with more downpours, all around the grey buildings dripped with dirty rainwater making even the bright signs seen dark and cold. I searched and searched to see something I could relate to, something to make me smile and I had almost given up hope when I saw him. Dripping wet and shivering he stood on the pavement opposite the gothic cathedral, he only smiled when he realised I had seen him. He was just what I needed, the only thing in the world that could make me smile that much, the only thing that could make me see sense. As I write in you, my trusted old friend from my room in a small B&B, wearing a dripping wet couture wedding dress I was right about something, I knew that today I would fulfil my destiny but only now as I recount what happened can I tell you that my destiny has yet to be written and that true love can take you anywhere.

Hears to many more adventures,
Miss Mary Marlborough

I apologise for not writing for a while, the adventure that is my life has continued in its dizzying spin. Since getting married a month ago in a small church in Wordsley Tom and I have been struggling; we have moved into this cottage which is where I now write from. Although I am enjoying the peace and quiet of the countryside it is nothing like Marlborough. I am miles away from home and I feel quite isolated. Tom has managed to secure a job as a delivery man for the local greengrocers but the wage is tiny, it barely covers the rent. After I left my first fiancé gawping at the altar, my father's butler managed to track me down and gave me some money (he had always been an ally) but now I have used all of the cash to secure the cottage and buy a small amount of furniture. My Father dis-inherited me when he disowned me after the wedding incident, not even my mother has tried to contact me. My life is not going the way I planned, I am making a small bit of money by cleaning clothes in our tiny kitchen but it is not what I'm used to, although I was tired of the finishing schools and gala events, I never thought the reality of leaving it would involve losing my trust fund. I love Tom more than anything but this is getting too hard, I don't know if I can survive without a safety net. I'm starting to wonder if love really is enough …
Sincerely,
Mrs Mary Palmer

Norma gently rested her Mother's tear stained diary on the edge of her disowned daughter's bed and started to cry, buried tears dropping like a waterfall onto the thick carpet, not relenting for anything. How could she have not known what her own mother had been through? The strength it took her to follow her heart, and to become her own person. Norma felt like a fraud, how could she have a mother that was so strong but allow herself to be so easily led? She had let her own daughter be driven away, while she stood and watched. She had always hoped that her mother was looking over her, but right now she hoped she wasn't, how would she ever explain to her why she had become this monster?!

Chapter 30

I had taken all of my exams and school was officially over. At this point, all of the people I had known at school had the next stage figured out but I wasn't one of them. I wasn't clever enough to go to university, not skilled enough for an apprenticeship, and not rich enough to buy my way into a career. I was officially in a rut and the summer heat wasn't helping either, as it made me feel lazy and lethargic. I had spent a week walking around town trying to find a job but all the summer work had been taken so I'd filled my time with cleaning and doing jobs around the house. Every afternoon I used to watch Mr Beautiful mow the lawn and paint the fence, but every day he looked more and more tired, we hadn't had a night out or any time together since Ian's party and that was starting to take its toll.

Rose had been keeping her son on a tight leash ever since that night in the car. Every time we tried to plan something she would come up with another job for him to do, I knew it was hard for him to say no to his mother but it was making me feel unwanted. Our first argument came when I had to go to the doctors for a check-up. Mr beautiful had a week's holiday, so I had asked him to come with me. On the morning of the appointment I knocked on his bedroom door, no answer, I'd gone downstairs, everywhere was silent, and then I checked outside, he wasn't there either. I was angry by this point, I had reminded him over dinner the night before and he said he was coming, now he was gone, no note, no nothing! So reluctantly, I pulled myself together and walked to the bus stop. By the time I reached the doctors, I was twenty minutes late, the price you pay for expecting someone to drive you. I sheepishly walked into the packed waiting room and explained my situation to the thirty something receptionist, who was sporting a horrible perm. "I understand" she said in her most patronising tone, "but the doctor has had to see his other patients, you can wait but it doesn't look good." I could feel steam coming from my ears "I'll just make another appointment" I said with a huff, then took the hint and left. By the time the dirty old bus eventually limped its way to my stop, I was seething, I sat down heavily on the seat and stared out of the grimy window, thinking of ways to kill my boyfriend. When I finally dismounted the moving sauna, my mood had gone from bad to worse, so you can imagine look on my face as I turned into the drive and saw Mr Beautiful weeding the borders.

"Are you alright Louise, you look angry?" he said as he stood to greet me.

"I take it you were busy this morning? I snapped "Taking your mother out, no doubt."

I stared at him for a few seconds, seeing his sweaty, shirtless body was doing nothing for me this morning so I continued to glare until he finally remembered.

"Was today your appointment?" he asked.

I nodded in agreement and started to walk past him. I was in no mood for his apology.

"My mom asked me to take her shopping early this morning, I completely forgot. I'm sorry"

I stopped in my tracks and turned back to him. This was it, I couldn't take anymore.

"That's convenient isn't it" I said sarcastically, "the one morning that she knows I want you to go with me. Sometimes I think you don't even know I'm here." I was shouting at him by now, but that didn't matter. "I play by all the rules, and I don't question anything … I help with the cleaning … the washing … the cooking, and all I wanted you to do was hold my hand at the doctors and you 'conveniently' forget."

By now he was getting angry.

"I think you're forgetting who put a roof over your head when you got kicked out, I had to put my neck on the line just to have you here. I think you should be a bit more grateful."

As soon as the words left his mouth, I could tell he regretted them, but it was too late, my head dropped down and I started to cry. As he tried to comfort me I pulled away and ran into the house. The room was hot and uncomfortable as I sat on my borrowed bed; tears pouring down my face as I wept uncontrollably. I had never felt more alone and un-wanted, and it was making me question all of my decisions. I had lied to my parents, and quit my job, all to fall in love with a man so he could reject me. When did I get so stupid?

I couldn't eat that day, and spent most of it in my borrowed room. It was 7:30 when my 'boyfriend' appeared in the doorway looking pale in the fading light.

"I wouldn't come any further" I said, not looking up "you don't want your head chopped off, it is on the line you know."

"My mom's not here, but I suppose I deserved that." he said, sounding defeated.

I still didn't look up as he moved next to my bed.

"Are you hungry? It's not like you to miss dinner."

"I didn't want to interrupt your cosy dinner with Rose; I would only cramp your style."

"Alright" he said raising his hand up. "I'm a crap boyfriend, I know. The last thing I want you to feel is unwanted, especially after what you've been through."

The room filled with an uncomfortable silence as he waited for my response. I didn't like being angry with him, and I could see the remorse in his face, but I was enjoying making him sweat a little.

I stared at him for a little longer until he started to really panic

"I'm sorry too; it's just these rules, and your mother, I've been feeling a bit neglected. I'll try my best to control my emotions more."

I could see his demeanour change as I spoke, colour started slowly coming back to his face, and he began to relax.

"I'm feeling that way too" he said, "it's hard being so close to you and not being able to do anything about it. I did deserve what you said earlier, I'm just not sure the street enjoyed it though; after you went inside, I saw the curtains twitching."

"That's all I need, more gossip from the neighbours" I said with a laugh. "I'll try and be angry at you inside the house from now on, how's that?"

He laughed and took me into his arms. I'd missed his touch, but my residual anger kept my feelings at bay. We spent the rest of the night talking, until Rose walked in at 10:30.

Chapter 31

Phillip sat at the dining nook in the corner of his kitchen looking at the result of the bomb that must have gone off. Tonight it was beef for tea and he could see Sharon cremating it on the stove. He didn't know how long the poor animal had been in the oven, but it looked like most of the day. Unfortunately cooking was not one of Sharon's better skills, although she did try hard, but nevertheless 'trying' had never been enough in the Fraser household, 'doing' and 'succeeding' were the only things that mattered. Mealtimes had once been his favourite time of the day, he would come home and his mother would have cooked a wonderful meal, but now he dreaded coming home. He was working Monday to Friday, nine until five every day to pay this mortgage but he never came home to a fulfilling meal. He didn't think Sharon was cut out to be a homemaker, unlike his wonderful mother.

Chapter 32

Somehow Norma's life continued as autumn began to bed in. Cold dark nights and even colder mornings were part of the course by late October. Michael had become even more distant over the summer so now they hardly spoke at all, and she felt so lonely. From time to time, she would turn to the diary just to feel close to her mother again, but mostly it made her feel even lonelier. Everytime she stood in her daughter's old room, a shiver would come over her, the small room felt sterile and fake. The old memories of putting her daughter to bed and reading her stories until she fell asleep in her arms had been pushed far from her mind. Now, all she could see was a sea of cold blue paint and cream carpet, a far cry from the warm and comforting pink it had been before.

One cloudy afternoon she had been reluctantly tidying the corner in the living room where her husband threw random papers when something caught her eye. The small book had become wedged between old gas and water bills so she picked it up but became instantly annoyed; it was Louise's bank book. The anger she had supressed deep down came flooding to the surface like a volcano. He had kicked her out without any money, or any access to money! How did he expect her to survive? Where did he expect her to go? How would she eat? She always knew he was a bastard but she had never thought he would be so heartless! She paced the room, her head spinning with the same questions … she had always hoped there was some part of him that loved them all, but she had been so wrong. Norma began checking the bank book, as if it would make her feel better. She hoped he had drawn out the money and packed it in one of her bags, but no. Why was she still giving him the benefit of the doubt? He had thrown the book on the floor and left it there, clearly not giving it a second thought. How long would it be before he did this to her? How long would it be until she was penniless and on the street?

The door opened at precisely 5:40pm but Norma had been sitting in the living room staring out of the window all afternoon. The dinner wasn't made, the kettle wasn't on, and the washing wasn't ironed. She counted Michael's footsteps as he walked through their home. One … two … three into the dining room, four … five … six down the hall and into the kitchen, seven … eight … nine into the living room, ten … eleven … twelve, she looked up as her husband leered over her. She clutched the last remaining link to her daughter as he tried to snatch it from her as if it was her last possession on earth. He began to shout but it made no difference, she held eye contact with him, even when he slapped her hard across the face. For the first time in her life, it didn't hurt. There was nothing he could do to her that he hadn't done already, and as he pulled her off the chair and yanked up her skirt she held onto the book and closed her eyes.

Chapter 33

If 1966 was the summer of celebration, 1976 was the summer of frustration. My relationship with Mr Beautiful was becoming more and more strained as the dark nights began to close in. The arguments that had started during the peak of the summer heat continued bubbling under the surface, as we both tried to mask our emotions with other activities. My search for a job had eventually resulted in part time work cleaning a large house a few streets away, twice a week. Mr Beautiful had eventually given in to his mother and now spent all his spare time doing jobs around the house. In an attempt to cure the boredom, I had taken up sewing. Making dresses and skirts had become an outlet for all the spare time I had, but I had found some pleasure in my weekly trips to the market for fabric. All in all, we were surviving. It was around this time that I started hearing the arguments. Mr Beautiful and his mother started having regular battles over money, and my lack of it. The arguments had been going on for two long weeks when I decided to take action.

I heard Mr Beautiful coming upstairs after one of the more lively spats. Despite his room being out of bounds when he was in there, I couldn't stay quiet anymore so I crossed the landing into the lions den. He was lying on his bed, staring at the ceiling, when he saw me, he immediately sat up and looked shocked.

"What are you doing Louise? You know the rules."

"I can't just sit in my room and let you take the flack for me; if my presence here is a problem, then I shall go."

I was angry and emotional as I spoke to him. I had been carried for too long, and it was time I took responsibility for myself.

"Where exactly would you go Louise, you have nothing?" he shot back. "You need to stay here, I won't let you go out on the streets, you won't survive!"

"Are you saying I can't look after myself? Because I can, and will, if I have to. I won't let you ruin your relationship with your mother because of me. I've been kicked out once, it won't hurt for it to happen again, at least this time I'll expect it."

We were mid argument when Rose burst through the door.

"You are not supposed to be in here, did I not make that clear?" she shouted at me. Her placid face was suddenly red and swollen with anger.

"I only came in to tell him I was leaving" I shouted as I stormed out of the door, and back across the landing.

Every emotion I had ever felt was now bursting through my body. I could hear the yelling coming from his room but it was all just noise to me. I grabbed my suitcase off the top of the wardrobe and started hurriedly throwing clothes into it. Under my angry demeanour, I was quivering like a little girl. Mr Beautiful was right, where would I go? I had no-one. I was sobbing over pleated skirts and silk shirt dresses when the door burst open. I felt his arms wrap around me and tried to shake him off but the more I shook, the tighter he held me, until I eventually gave in. My body was lifeless as he supported all my weight against his chest. I didn't know if this was the beginning or the end, but I couldn't let go. After what seemed like a lifetime, he lifted me up and lay me down on the bed. I could feel the lid of my suitcase under my back as he eased my head onto the pillow.

"There's no need to cry anymore, it's all going to be fine, please trust me."

He spoke gently to me, as I tried to resist his charms.

"But what about your mom, I can't …" he wouldn't let me finish my sentence.

"You leave her to me" he said, "I'm a grown man, and it's time I started acting like one."

Chapter 34

As Christmas Eve descended, Phillip and Sharon were being handed glasses of champagne by the hired help from a large round table in the hall at her parents' house on the outskirts of town. Family portraits smiled back at him everytime he turned, as if laughing at him in his shiny car dealer's suit. As they moved around the house, its lavishness became clear, every room had a feature fireplace with huge marble surround, heavy draped velvet curtains in deep greens and gold framed bay windows., Elaborate Persian rugs in burgundy and green dominated each large living space. The opulence took Phillip by surprise, and suddenly he became aware of how ordinary he really was. He had always believed he was from an upper class family but the three bed semi he grew up in hardly compared to this.

He spent most of the night stuck with men in their late fifties talking about stocks, shares and investments, he had none of the above, so had looked a fool several times when his opinion was asked. The icing on the cake came, when one of the men recognised him; it seems Phillip had sold his wife a car. This provided a great laugh for the large group of men that now surrounded him, so feeling inadequate and down-trodden, Phillip found his father-in-law's study and poured himself a large brandy. Sitting in the large chesterfield setee that completely engulfed his wispy frame, he suddenly realised how unimportant he really was.

Later that night, Phillip Fraser was sitting on his bed when his wife glided in wearing a sheer pink baby doll negligée, her blonde hair pulled back off her face revealing her stunning features. He knew what he should be feeling right now, but he couldn't get excited. Despite the attractiveness of his wife, he was no longer aroused by her. She climbed onto the bed and crawled on top of him, grinding across his body. When they were first married, he loved making love to her, but now it had become monotonous and boring, he was just thankful it was getting less frequent. The only other reason why he was struggling to get aroused was Sharon's longing for a baby, but the thought of this scared him to death. He was not ready for children, he still felt young and he had recently started a flirtation with a teller at the bank. He closed his eyes and thought about the bank girl as he made robotic love to his wife.

Chapter 35

The first time I noticed winter had well and truly gone was on April the 1st, I sat up in my borrowed bed and looked up at the curtains to see the sun pushing against them. As soon as I opened them, the small bedroom became flooded with light, renewing me with a new energy. Thankfully over the last few months I had managed to acquire a few more houses to clean, so with last week's wages burning a hole in my pocket I ventured to the Wolverhampton market fabric stalls. When I arrived at the bus stop, across from the bustling market I noticed that everyone had been bitten by the spring bug. The familiar outside stalls filled with their tempting fruits and vegetables glistened in the morning sun, and that sweet aroma began to fill the air once again. As I ventured past the lively market traders, I entered the slightly more sombre inside market. Reams and reams of delicate fabrics lined the walkways, obscuring my view to the next stand. Despite how familiar the market was to me, when I was here alone it had a completely different feeling. Unable to choose from the hundreds of different fabrics that swung around the stalls I was wandering around aimlessly, taking in the atmosphere when I felt a tap on my shoulder, I swung round as if I had just been woken from a dream to find my old 'best' friend standing behind me.

Angela was exactly like I remembered her, minus the crowd of boys hanging off her every word. She was dressed in a navy blue jacket and skirt which looked like it was from a building society, and she was carrying a heavy looking satchel.

"Fancy seeing you here" Angela said to me in her perky tone.

"I could say the same to you" I replied "how have you been?"

"Oh you know, good, bad, indifferent. How are you? You look great, I love your outfit."

"Thank you, I've started making my own clothes. I'm ok though, you know good, bad, indifferent."

After a few more minutes of small talk, Angela had to get off to work but not before I could invite her out on Saturday so we could catch up properly. She gladly accepted my invite and we went our separate ways. I then forced myself to make a decision on fabric and headed home.

At 12:30 on Saturday afternoon I was walking down the stairs, ready to leave for my shopping excursion. I was wearing a knee length shirt dress with three quarter sleeves that I had made out of royal blue fabric. I had even added a belt after it looked a little shapeless. It felt good to be going out with a friend, finally another girl to talk to. When I went outside to tell Mr Beautiful I was leaving, he was mowing the lawn without a shirt on, and looked magnificent. The sun was glistening off the sweat on his muscled shoulders, and he looked tanned in the amber light. I stood and stared for a few moments before he turned around.

"I'm off now to meet Angela" I said, as I walked towards him.

He looked shocked, as if he didn't know what was going on.

"I told you the other day, we have a shopping date." I explained for the second time this week.

"I don't remember you telling me, I thought we might spend the afternoon together."

I was surprised by his reaction, he seemed moody, not his normal self.

"You didn't say you wanted to go out, you haven't even spoken to me this morning." I said, as I started to get frustrated. "I can't cancel on Angela now; she'll think I'm so rude."

"I didn't think I had to book you so far in advance, enjoy your afternoon, I'll just stay here by myself."

I stood there open-mouthed as I tried to figure out what was happening. This was another side to his character I had yet to see.

"I'm going to ignore your sarcasm, and go out with my friend." I said, my sunny mood disappearing. "Enjoy your garden."

I could sense his shock as I turned and walked away. His tone had changed when he began calling my name, but I still ignored him, the last thing we needed was another argument for the neighbours to talk about.

My 'date' with Angela turned out to be four hours of us sitting in Beatties café drinking cups of tea and talking about boys. She too was having parent trouble after her mom had caught her in bed with her boyfriend, apparently he didn't take kindly to being kicked out of her house and was now seeing another girl with much looser morals. When it was my turn to talk, she sat in awe as I went over the last year's goings on, not leaving anything out.

"Wow Louise I never knew anything had happened, my mom sees Norma every week at the market and she hasn't said anything. Are you having any contact with them at all?"

"No, they've cut me out completely; I didn't even have any money when they kicked me out. All my money was in the building society and my dad kept the book. I was completely broke until I managed to get this little job cleaning houses."

Angela's mouth was wide open as I recounted my sad tale, and even when I left her that day, I still don't think she totally believed me. Despite the fright I'd given my old friend, it felt good to have told someone, I didn't feel alone anymore and that was empowering.

As I walked back into the house I heard the television go quiet and Mr Beautiful appeared in the hallway. I looked at him with my new devil may care attitude, and it took him by surprise.

"How was shopping?" he asked with a subdued tone.

"We didn't do much shopping actually; we just talked about how annoying boys are."

He started to say he was sorry, again, but I stopped him.

"Listen" I said, "you can say sorry all you like, but I won't be treated like a little girl that's got to be constantly at your beck and call, I'd have gone back home if that was the case."

I was staring him down and I could tell I was winning.

"You're right" he said "I'm sorry I made you feel like that, especially as you had told me. How about you spend the rest of the day with me, I was thinking dinner out maybe? You could wear one of your designs."

"Well as you asked so nicely, I suppose I could find room in my schedule." I said, as I moved towards him, "I'll assume it's on you?"

He grinned as he took me into his arms. "Not a problem, I have to admit though, the strong woman side to you really turns me on, maybe we won't make the restaurant?" he winked at me as he pulled my hips into him and I could feel him getting hard inside his jeans, it was turning me on.

"I'm sorry" I said as I pulled away "but I'm a lady you know, and we don't go in for things like that."

My confidence was at an all-time high as I walked away from him, and I could feel him staring at my bum as I started my swagger up the stairs.

"You may pick me up at my room at 7pm" I told him as I climbed the stairs, his eyes still on me. I think when I turned and winked at him at the top, I pretty much finished him off.

Inside my room I shut the door and smiled to myself, I loved the new me.

Chapter 36

Norma was standing at the butcher's stall inside Wolverhampton market. As she waited for her number to be called, she couldn't help but notice that two women were staring at her. Ignoring their glares, she continued about her business. It was only when she had finished all her shopping that she noticed another two ladies staring at her, one of which was Angela's mom. This annoyed Norma enormously, she was not used to being the subject of gossip. Taking a deep breath, she confronted the two fat women that were standing to the left of her. Much to her surprise the two 'fat ducks' began to waddle away, "Cowards" she thought to herself. After contemplating whether to follow them or not, she decided against it and walked home. What a strange morning she thought, what could they be gossiping about?

Chapter 37

Thankfully my birthday came and went without much fuss, unlike the previous year. It felt good to turn nineteen though, and it made me think of my mother. I missed her every day but I couldn't risk going to see her, the thought that she may reject me was too much for me to bear.

I had just got home from work on a Monday afternoon in late May when the doorbell rang, just as I'd started sipping my long awaited cup of tea. It took a lot of energy to pull myself off the sofa but eventually I lazily heaved open the front door to be greeted by the last person I expected to see.

My mother was standing in the small porch. I was too gobsmacked to know what to say so we just stood there in silence for a few minutes until eventually I spoke:

"What are you doing here?" I said in my bemused tone. "Actually, how do you know I'm here?" I asked, as my confusion grew.

"Rose came to see me. She told me she was worried about you, she's a sweet woman and thought it wasn't right that a girl of your age should be without her mother." Norma explained.

"May I come in? Then we can talk properly."

I stood silently for a moment, my head was spinning, but I was missing her so I conceded.

Luckily the house would be empty for another three hours, so at least we could talk privately. My mother turned down the drink I offered her and took a seat on the large setee. She sat perfectly up-right in her navy blue skirt suit, and seemed very uneasy. I don't think either of us knew where to start so we sat in silence for another few minutes. After adjusting her posture, my mother broke the silence.

"I know I did wrong Louise, by letting your father abandon you, but you have to understand how much you hurt him that day?"

I was gobsmacked, why should I feel bad about hurting him?

"So let me get this straight, he spent five years abusing and hurting me, while you stood idly by, but when I do it back I should feel sorry. I don't think so."

My mom looked taken aback by my new attitude.

"He is willing to let you come back home if you just apologise, it took a lot of convincing for him to go back on what he said Louise."

I was so angry that I shouted the response.

"If you think I even want to come home, you are very, very wrong! I will never apologise to that tyrant, not as long as I live! You should have stood up for me, but you can never do that, can you? How do you think I would feel? What do you think coming home would do to me? What do you think he would do to me the next time I step out of line? He wanted me out, he's got his wish. Now it's your turn to be kicked out of somewhere. Please leave!"

My mother was shocked and clearly upset by my comments, but that didn't bother me.

"Leave now!" I shouted again, this time standing up and walking towards the door.

As she stood, she avoided eye contact with me and quietly walked into the hallway. She was standing in the porch when she tried to say something else; but I had heard enough and closed the door in her face. I stood watching as the outline of her body moved away from the door and walked up the drive. All of my emotions and hormones were raging around my body, so I turned and slid myself down the front door until I hit the floor.

I don't know how long I'd been crying when I heard Mr Beautiful's car pull into the drive, so hauling myself up I dragged my seized body into the back room. I purposely avoided his gaze when he walked in but it didn't take long for him to figure out why. I could feel how red and sore my eyes were as he peered into them. "Have you been crying?" he asked, sounding concerned. I told him I'd just got a bit of a cold, and that he wasn't to worry. I don't think he believed me, but he didn't push it, he could tell I wasn't in the mood to talk. After my boyfriend told me about his day, I excused myself and went upstairs.

I sat on the bed, I couldn't stop replaying the conversation I'd had earlier. The fact she thought I would just come home and apologise was ridiculous. It was just at that moment I realised it was time to get going with my life, after all I'd already come so far.

Chapter 38

Rose couldn't sleep. Despite the late hour, her eyes were wide open and staring up at the ceiling. It didn't matter how she lay, her body just wouldn't settle, but unfortunately for Rose she knew why sleep eluded her. Why had she ever gone to that house? It felt so cold when she sat in their living room, and Norma seemed so distant. This was unsettling to Rose as she was used to families being so close, after all her mother hadn't even wanted her to leave aged thirty when she finally got married. The worst thing to happen though was today, Louise had clearly been upset and she didn't even comfort her. After all she had said to Norma about a girl needing her mother, she still couldn't lower her guard and be the mother figure.

Chapter 39

That summer was hottest in a decade, and it had started out great. I was taking regular walks through Manor Park, and had even started going to cafes in town by myself. The warmth had brought out my creative gene and I was sewing summery dresses by the truck load. Unfortunately, by the end of August, we'd all had enough of summer, every day was at least 32 degrees, and there wasn't a breeze to be found. One Sunday afternoon I was lying on the bed with the small window wide open, the close heat was sending my hormones raging, which in turn was making me anxious. I was longing for some alone time with Mr Beautiful but he was working so much overtime that we hardly saw each other. I longed to feel close to him again like we did that afternoon in the library, but that felt like such a long time ago now, almost like it was some kind of wonderful dream. As I closed my eyes, I tried to go back to those times, but the more I tried, the more my head became filled with the reality of what being with Mr Beautiful was really like. Stupid real life … always getting in the way. I lay there for the rest of the day, unable to get out of my own head. Thoughts had become merged into one big annoyance, and made my brain feel like a ticking time bomb. Thankfully, I had not had another visit from my mother but the last one still played on my mind. Over the past months I had tried to rationalise the reason for her visit.

First: how did she know where I was?

Second: was it a coincidence at the time she showed up? Or did she know what time I'd be back?

Third: would Mr Beautiful have gone to see her?

Despite the clarity, I knew the answers would bring me, I was finding it hard to delve any deeper, the thought of being disappointed by the love of my life again was filling me with fear. However, I knew what I had to do. That evening we had sausage and mash for tea, not my favourite, especially when it is 30 degrees outside. We were all sat around the small, round table in the front room but despite the bright sunshine blazing through the bay window, the atmosphere felt cold and on edge so after ten minutes of uncomfortable silence, I took a deep breath and started my interrogation.

"My mother came here a few months ago" I started to say. "She said that I would be allowed home if I apologised, but I declined her offer." Neither Rose nor her son would look at me, as they pushed burnt sausages around their plates. "I was shocked that she knew where I was, I don't remember being given the chance to leave a forwarding address when I was mercilessly kicked out."

I had just dropped a bomb in the middle of the table, so I sat there silently waiting for it to go off, but I think it had rendered them mute and paralysed because I couldn't even see them blinking.

I started on the re-fire. "I find it strange that there is only one person here who actually knows where I lived, and yet he is silent." I was staring at my boyfriend until he eventually lifted his head.

"It's not what you think" he said, "we were both concerned about you, and at your age it's important to have someone you can speak to. My mom went to speak with Norma to see if she could bring her around but it didn't work the way we had planned."

I was now staring at Rose but she wouldn't look back at me. "How dare you! This is not any of your business. I'm not surprised it didn't work out, they are only concerned with their own image, why do you think I was kicked out in the first place?!"

Turning to Mr Beautiful I asked him why he had not just had the balls to talk to me, but he couldn't think of a real explanation, he just sat there looking guilty.

"To say I'm angry is an understatement, if the two of you are so concerned about me, then stop giving me the cold shoulder and actually make me feel wanted."

I stood up from the table and stormed out of the room. I felt propelled to the front door so I grabbed a cardigan and left, slamming the door behind me.

Chapter 40

It took an hour of walking for me to notice how beautiful the evening was. The sun was starting to set and was casting an orange glow over all the trees in the park so I sat on a bench and took in a deep breath. As my head rolled towards the sky I became mesmerised by the changing colours dancing above my head, red, orange and yellow swirls filled the sky and looked as though they may catch fire at any moment. I felt so at peace here, I didn't want to go back. Maybe I could run forever, the amazing romantic notion that life could be that simple, filled my head and made my eyes close. When I finally woke the sky was dark blue and full of stars. I jumped up and tried to remember where I was, found my bearings and started walking back. The atmosphere was so different on the return journey. The rows of houses that lined the back streets of Penn looked identical in the dark light and seemed never ending. As I walked the eerie streets, I realised my mind was suddenly clearer. Maybe realising my fears was not as scary as I thought.

When I entered the dark house, I saw Mr Beautiful sitting on the stairs. His face looked even more worried in the grey, shadowy hallway.

"I was five minutes away from going to find you" he said in a hushed tone.

"Well no need, I'm here now." I replied sternly.

"I think we should talk about this Louise, I want to explain."

"What is there to explain? Instead of coming and talking to me, you sent Rose to see my mother, two women who go out of their way to make me feel unwanted sitting in the same room. You couldn't even warn me she was coming, I had to be surprised by it, and then to not even bring it up afterwards, that was just horrible. You were supposed to protect and stand by me, not keep quiet and hope it all blows over."

My mind was clear as I spoke, I didn't feel angry, just disappointed.

I walked past him and into the kitchen where I was sipping a glass of water when he appeared in the doorway.

"When I first met you I thought I knew how to behave, but I realise now how naïve I was. I pretend to be this big, confident guy but inside I'm terrified of making a mistake. I've never been in this kind of relationship before; I've always been more of a 'get-in-get-out' sort of guy, excuse the pun. Please don't give up on me Louise, I am trying to do the right thing, this whole situation isn't perfect for me either."

I stood and looked at him; despite my current feelings I couldn't help but admire him and in the moonlight he looked so handsome. I wanted to believe him more than anything but I'd been let down too many times before, why should I believe he's any different?

"I'm trying, but you're not making it easy. Everytime we fight you tell me it won't happen again, but a few months later it starts all over. The back and forth is killing me, I'm starting to wonder why I should believe you."

He was silent as I walked past him, and up into the small bedroom. Thankfully the window was still open and the bed sheets were cool on my naked skin. Despite the clarity of my mind, sleep didn't come easily and I tossed and turned for what felt like hours until I finally settled.

I was woken early in the morning by the rain coming down outside, it was a wonderful sound and the air already felt fresher. As I watched it slowly stop the glorious sun reflected off the puddles and everywhere seemed so bright. Looking out over the dazzling car roofs and pink, blue and orange flowers my mind became instantly made up. I would give Mr Beautiful another chance, after all without him, I would have nowhere to live.

Chapter 41

Phillip sat on the end of his bed chewing at the fat around his fingernails as Sharon was in the bathroom taking a pregnancy test. He could feel his heartbeat pulsating through his body as he tried to calm his nerves, he didn't want a child, especially with his wife; after all she could barely look after him. His wife walked into the room holding the white stick in her hands and joined him on the edge of the bed. He knew Sharon was nervous but it was for a different reason, she wanted a baby. The three minutes went by so slowly and the silence was getting un-bearable. When the timer went off it sent shockwaves through Phillips body, Sharon grabbed his hand and they both squeezed as she slowly turned it over …

Negative! She wasn't pregnant! Phillip was doing somersaults inside, and was trying to control the urge to smile. Sharon was crying, he did his best to comfort her but she must have felt that it wasn't genuine. After a while, Phillip tucked his emotional wife into bed, and made an excuse to leave the house. He drove for fifteen minutes until he reached the other side of Wolverhampton, the area was well known because of its high crime rate. He pulled up his car outside the terraced house with the red front door … number 36. As he got out, he could feel eyes watching him, so he hurriedly locked his luxurious car and made his way up the tidy front path. Number 36 was the nicest house on the street (but that wasn't saying much). The front lawn was mowed and the windows and door looked freshly painted. Inside he could see the curtains were drawn, but he expected that. As instructed, he knocked three times and waited for a response.

Amy of number 36 was dressed in a black baby doll with red ribbon, and her long brown hair was draped over one shoulder. After welcoming him in, she asked if he would like a drink, which he gladly accepted. Amy made a few moments of small talk before she delicately took his hand and lead him upstairs. The house was nicely decorated if not a little plain. The walls were white but there were no family photos, or trinkets and all the carpets seemed new and were a deep shag pile. Although it looked nice on the surface, the paint and carpets felt like they were masking something a lot more sinister. Upstairs there were four brown doors, each one closed. Phillip followed his hostess into the one at the front of the house. Inside the room dark red candles were burning and in the dim light, he could see heavy damask curtains in burgundy blocking any light from outside. The room was sparse with only a bed, dressing table and chair. Amy sat him down on the red wine coloured duvet and asked him to wait. He sat patiently as she firmly shut the door. The linen below him felt cool, and of good quality, but this was not enough to calm his nerves. As Amy walked towards him, he was trying to avoid eye contact but before he could object she was sitting on his lap and pushing his head up to meet her gaze. He had to admit, she was pretty and he was very aroused by her, but he still couldn't believe he had come here. She told him to relax and he did what he was told, Amy then began to un-button his shirt.

With every button she revealed more of his chest and began slowly teasing and caressing his nipples. She moved down his body and un-did his belt … gently pulling out his crisp, white shirt and removing it from his shoulders allowing it to flutter to the floor. Standing up, Amy pulled him up with her and starting at his shoulders and working slowly down his torso she lightly nibbled at his skin until she reached his crotch. She tugged firmly on his hard leather belt and it ran quickly through the holes and lightly whipped it onto the floor causing him to jump. Her large brown eyes moved down his neglected and un-toned body, as she dropped to her knees and began to un-do his trousers. Pulling his tailored navy blue trousers and crisp white underwear to the floor, she revealed his erect penis. This seemed to please her, and she began to tease his man hood with her tongue, slowly tickling the tip with the end of her tongue making him quiver, and then lightly sucking and nibbling making him groan. When she started kissing the shaft, she pushed him back onto the bed and continued, while massaging the inside of his thighs with her hands. He had never been so turned on and had to stop himself from cumming a few times. Everytime he tensed his body, she eased up but then would start again, until the pressure inside him was un-bearable. Sensing this, she stopped and climbed onto his body, easing herself onto him and rocking back and forth. She felt warm and tight as she rode him then he began to get the familiar feeling back again. This time he could not stop it, he came hard and fast as his body tensed up but she went quicker and pressed her chest onto his forcing him down. The burst came out of him like a volcano but she pinned him down harder, it wasn't until his whole body had relaxed that she let him go, and climbed off him.

Phillip lay on the bed momentarily dazed. Amy was already pulling on a dressing gown and blowing out the candles and as she turned on the light, his eyes started to focus. The room suddenly felt cold and dirty. The magnolia walls were empty and emotionless, and the luxury bed linen felt colder than before. As he looked over, he could see Amy sitting with her back to him at the dressing table. He could see her reflection in the mirror but without make up she looked tired, empty and older than her years.

Unable to do anything, he put the money on the bed and left.

Chapter 42

Winter had finally arrived and the stifling heat of the summer and constant rain of the autumn had been replaced by clear blue skies and frosty mornings, I loved this time of year. I was now working full time after picking up a few more houses to clean. One morning I was running late and had forgotten to wash the clothes I normally went to work in, so without any other option I had to put on the blue flares and cream blouse I had just made. The first house I was cleaning today was located about half a mile from where I was living. Occupying a large corner plot, the house had crisp white render on the outside, a sweeping driveway that went all around the front and a large privet hedge to stop anyone from peeking in. The lady of the house was Mrs Windsor and her husband had made his money in toy shops (he had twenty of them). As normal, I rang the doorbell and was greeted by Mrs Windsor herself. She was always polite, and asked me how I was but normally that was as far as it went, today was different.

I hung my coat up on the large coat rack in the corner of the spacious hall and asked Mrs Windsor for an apron; it was then that she stopped and looked at me. Normally she wouldn't give me a second look but today she was looking me up and down as if I was made of gold. I stood there confused and worried so I asked again for an apron.

"I'm sorry Louise but that outfit, where did you get it?"

"Oh this, I made it, it's a bit of a hobby of mine."

"It looks lovely, you really did this yourself?"

She seemed confused and she wasn't the only one.

"I'm sorry to wear it but I forgot to wash my other clothes, I've just been so busy you see … if I could just have that apron then I can start cleaning."

I soon realised that Mrs Windsor had other ideas. She grabbed my hand and led me into the large living room. As I stood there, she looked closely at what I was wearing, asking me to lift my arms up and un-tucking my blouse, the crazy lady then asked me to wait while she made a phone call. Standing in the opulent living space I felt completely bemused, all around me were large pieces of squidgy furniture and an abundance of lamps. Everything from the curtains to the carpet were cream and gold, but somehow today I felt afraid to touch anything.

"I'm so sorry about all this Louise, will you sit down for a moment, I want to talk to you about something."

I sat down and began to worry.

"Mrs Windsor, I'm sorry to ruin your plan, but I do have other houses to get to, so I really should start cleaning."

"Who else are you cleaning for today" the crazy lady asked me.

When I had told her she promptly walked off and didn't return for another ten minutes.

Over the next half an hour, two more ladies that I cleaned for arrived and were excitedly shown into the living room, gripping mugs of tea.

"Louise I'm sorry for the confusion, you obviously know Mrs Green, and Mrs Woodhall."

In my confused state I nodded and shuffled to the edge of my seat.

"Louise I think your outfit is very good and so do these two ladies'. The three of us have wanted to start our own business for a long time but have been struggling to find the people with the right talent to help us. We think you might be that person. Do you have more creations at home or is this the first one?"

I sat completely motionless, in an utter state of shock. I finally managed to tell them that I had more where I was living, and then went back into shock. The three women were grinning at me like Cheshire cats and I felt completely overwhelmed.

"I have cancelled your other jobs for today Louise, so would you mind bringing them to show us, we'd love to see them?"

Still dazed I nodded my head, and managed to mumble a 'yes' before I headed for the door.

The rest of the day was a blur, I took over all of my designs and they seemed to love them all, I even had to model a lot of them. By the time my back was planted on my borrowed bed, I was in an even bigger state of shock. The business was built around a growing trade for custom made outfits for well-to-do ladies in the surrounding areas apparently being very well dressed herself, a lot of rich wives would ask Mrs Windsor for shops and stylists to use for important events. She soon saw this as a lucrative business idea and had been looking for a dressmaker ever since. The deal was, that the ladies would discuss with Mrs Windsor what they wanted to wear, I would draw the design, and then the lady would pay up front; I would then take the money for material plus a 20 % cut as wages. It seemed too good to be true, but we did have meetings set up already for Friday so I was just going to go for it. Hoping it was time for the tides to change.

Chapter 43

Mr Beautiful sat on his bed holding his certificate in his hand, He had passed his apprenticeship and was now fully qualified as a machine operator for Goodyear. Nobody knew he had passed as it was a few months early, but that's why he had been putting in all the extra hours. The job he had accepted was great money but it was three shifts, mornings, afternoons and nights. He hoped Louise would be alright with this because all he wanted to do was support her but he was more than aware of the pressure that the recent long hours had put on their relationship. When she had started this new business with Mrs Windsor he had been so proud of her but now he felt like she was leaving him behind, he had trouble understanding why she needed to work so much. He hoped that after January 1st, all this would change and he would have his girlfriend's attention well and truly back on him.

Chapter 44

New Year's Eve morning had arrived and it was my first day off since the business had started. I was taking advantage of this down time by lying on my bed staring up at the ceiling and allowing my mind to wander. My relationship with Mr Beautiful had become increasingly strained over the last few months, it seemed the busier and more successful the business became the more distant he had become. I started to weep as I wondered how long we would last, now that I was becoming more financially independent and no longer needed to be under his Mother's roof, were we willing to fight for us? Or had we just grown apart? As these questions filled my mind I heard a knock on my door. "Come in" I said as the door slowly opened, Mr Beautiful was standing nervously in the doorway so I asked him what he needed. "Would you like to come out with me tonight, to a gala dinner in town? Its black tie, I thought you might like the opportunity to dress up." I agreed to go with him and he nervously backed out of the doorway, shutting the door behind him.

The house remained empty all day, I knew Rose had gone to her friends, so she had wished me happy New Year this morning. Mr Beautiful did not return until 7pm, by which time I was standing waiting. In an attempt to save what was left of our relationship I had worn a dress I'd made purely for a special occasion. Back in November I had been shopping for other material when a new fabric caught my eye. It was a shimmery pale pink with gold flecks running down the pleats; which I had made into a one shoulder, Grecian style evening gown. The stunning ensemble was tight at the top, then the pleated material flared out at the waist in a floor length, two layer A-line skirt. It was my best creation, and hopefully it was enough. My hair was half up half down, and I was wearing gold T-bar shoes. As Mr Beautiful opened the front door he looked gorgeous in a black dinner suit complete with bow tie, and the shiniest shoes I had ever seen. He took one look at me and appeared to melt, his eyes lit up and I knew that my plan had worked, at least for the moment.

The hotel was called The Connaught and was situated in the centre of town. As we pulled up, people were already milling excitedly around the entrance and in the hallway. The atmosphere in town was electric and I could tell this was going to be an amazing night. As Mr beautiful got out of the car, the valet opened the door for me and I linked arms with my boyfriend. When we made our entrance into the wood panelled bar, it was full of well-dressed guests sipping champagne and eating canapés who were giving us admiring looks as we walked along the parke flooring towards the main ballroom. I felt a strange sense of déjà vu as I glided alongside my dashing companion, but upon catching my reflection in the gold framed mirror, I remembered when I was last here.

Ten years ago father had bought us here for a family dinner to celebrate Phillip's birthday, I sat in the corner wearing a church outfit and nobody spoke to me but tonight couldn't be more different. Every man and woman was staring at me as I walked confidently through the decadent building. I even heard well dressed women commenting on my dress and asking their husbands why theirs weren't as good. "If only you'd come to see me", I whispered under my breath as I smiled broadly on my boyfriend's arm.

The main ballroom was large and opulent. Giant chandeliers hung from the ceiling and red and gold damask curtains framed large paned windows. There was an impressive, highly polished dance floor drawing my eye to the centre of the room. Mr Beautiful gave his name to the hostess and we were guided to our table, one of the twelve edging the dance floor, with six other people joining us, all couples. It was decorated beautifully with gold and cream, accented by crystal glasses. The main centrepiece of each table was a large display of white roses, gold pine cones and large green leaves that supported the base. They looked magnificent, like something that James Bond would see in a fancy casino.

As the night progressed, we drank champagne and ate wonderfully large prawns and velvety fillet steak topped with rich pate. By the time coffee was served, our table hummed with electricity and laughter. When the dancing started at around 10pm, Mr Beautiful and I were the first on the dance floor. He took me into his arms and swirled me around the highly polished floor, he never stopped looking into my eyes and I remembered how it felt to be completely in love.

"You do love me, don't you Louise?" he asked when we finally slowed our dancing.

"Of course I do, you just don't make it easy sometimes."

"I know, I don't mean to, but I promise you it's going to get better, a lot better."

I laughed a little "you've said that before" I said, not quite convinced.

Then my world stopped spinning, however the other dancers didn't. Loved up couples continued to swirl around us to the quickening beat of the music, oblivious to what was happening. Mr Beautiful was on one knee in the middle of them all.

"Louise Fraser, I love you more than anything in the world, you have turned my life upside-down. Will you marry me?"

Chapter 45

The ballroom continued in its dizzying spin, purple, blue and red dresses blew around us as though we weren't there. Mr Beautiful's eyes were the most alluring I had ever seen them, glinting gold in the sparkling surroundings. In his hands was a magnificent diamond solitaire ring that looked more than he could afford. Every emotion I had ever felt was racing through my body as I thought out my response. Was I ready for marriage? What if he only became more distant? What if he became my father? I remembered the look in my mother's eyes on the day she married Michael, so adoring, what if this was the same situation? He hadn't moved since he said the words but I could tell his face was starting to expose his feelings, could I break his heart? Could I break mine?

His hands and face started to drop and I could see the pain running through him. I loved this man too much to hurt him; I stopped thinking of the negatives. Bending down I pulled his hands back up and he immediately met my gaze.

"Ask me again" I said excitedly.

He paused for a second and smiled, "Louise Fraser will you marry me?"

I instantly cried out "YES" and he proudly put the ring on my finger. I felt the electricity pass through my body as he slid on the gold and diamond ring. I had never felt more of a woman than I did right now. All around us people had caught on to what was happening and began to cheer in unison. Mr Beautiful held me tightly into him, then lifted me up and span me around. I could see smiling faces all around us as he effortlessly moved me; I buried my face into his shoulders and closed my eyes.

The rest of the night passed in a blur, people were congratulating us everywhere we turned, until, eventually it was just us. As Big Ben had struck midnight, we were sitting in the quiet garden at the back of the Connaught Hotel. No one else was there, it was just us. My future husband had his arm around me and I was pressed right up against his side with my head resting on his shoulder.

"At least you can stop working all those hours, now you've got me to look after you" Mr Beautiful said

"What do you mean? Why would I stop working?" I responded, feeling slightly shocked.

"Well, I've been offered a full contract now so I can cover all our bills, and whatever other things you might want."

I sat there wondering where my perfect moment had gone, I had worked so hard, why would I throw it all away to be a housewife? Had I just made a terrible mistake?

Chapter 46

I sat at the small dining table and looked blankly at the empty piece of paper in front of me. I knew I had to carry on but I didn't where to start.

17 Maple Crescent,
Wolverhampton,
West Midlands,
WV6 0NP.
10th January 1978

Dear Mother,
It is with great happiness, and sadness that I write to you. I wanted to inform you that on New Year's Eve I got engaged. However, despite this letter I want you to know that the events of recent years have not been forgotten. Despite this, if there is any chance that you and I can become part of each other's lives again during this period I would be grateful.
I am sorry for the way I acted towards you the last time we met, however I wanted to make my feelings clear. I know now that you were not to blame for the way I was treated but there will be a part of me that still resents you for allowing it to happen, I don't think that will ever change. Despite this I need you now more than ever to help me through to the next stage of my life.
Regards,
Louise

As I folded up the letter that would surely send a shockwave through the Fraser household I considered not going through with it, but thankfully good sense prevailed. As I got off the bus in my old neighbourhood, I felt a definite feeling of discomfort, the wounds of that night were still raw as I cautiously walked up the winding street. I saw my old home loom in the distance, I became even more anxious. My father's car was on the drive and the curtains were open so I considered turning back, but this was something I needed to do. I hurriedly walked up the drive keeping out of the view of the window and quietly posted the letter through the red front door that had once been so familiar. Time stood still as I listened to the letter hit the dark green mat that stood just a few inches away from me and gave me instant flashbacks to that night. I decided to turn my back on the front door and the painful memories and walked away down the frost covered path.

Chapter 47

Norma Fraser was sitting on the floor in her daughter's old room with her writing pad in one hand, and life changer in the other. Earlier that day she had found the hand-delivered letter on the mat and couldn't believe her eyes when she read who it was from, the thought that Louise had been here made her feel warm inside, but there was an undertone in the letter that made her feel un-easy about her daughter's situation. Despite the un-ease she felt under the surface, the letter comforted her, so she gripped it tightly as she replayed the scene from Christmas day. The walls of her little girl's room were still alive with the argument that Norma still couldn't believe had taken place.

5 Common walk,
Penn,
Wolverhampton,
West Midlands,
WV4 8LP
16th January 1978

Dear Louise,
The news of your engagement is wonderful, and has made me smile for the first time in months. However, this letter is tinged with sadness as I must tell you of the breakdown of your brother's marriage. As a Christmas present, your father had presented Phillip and Sharon with a nursery at our house for what he hoped would be an impending baby. This however backfired. I feel as though this is slightly my fault, as I knew something was wrong, but I refused to acknowledge it.
I was putting the finishing touches to my festive dinner when the shouting started, a few minutes later Sharon ran down the stairs and out of the house, I ran out of the kitchen and found Sharon

crying outside, one hour later the truth was out in the open. It seems that Phillip has been unhappy in his marriage for quite some time and does not want to start a family with anyone, especially Sharon. The presentation of the room sent Phillip into panic and forced him to reveal his true feelings to his wife, who stormed out and is now living back with her parents. Phillip is still living at his house but he is a regular guest here.

As you can imagine, your father has not taken the news well and has not been into work since, instead opting to sit in his chair all day, every day.

I understand your feelings towards us, and why you acted the way you did, but I also miss you deeply, and hope that even in a small way I can be involved in this special time in your life.

Love,

Mom x

Chapter 48

A month had passed since Mr Beautiful's gallant proposal and we were standing at the blood red door. On the outside everything seemed the same, but we knew that inside was a very different story. As the key began to turn I began to panic, and tried to run away but my fiancé held my hand so tightly I couldn't. My mother appeared in the doorway looking relieved to see us, and immediately invited us in. The house was immaculate as usual, despite the recent events, my mother wouldn't allow her house to fall into disarray. She led us through to the dining room where Phillip and father were both seated. I could feel the chill coming from the table already, only my mother had acknowledged our presence but we expected that. After a few minutes of uncomfortable silence and tea pouring my father got down to business.

"Despite your mother's excitement about this forthcoming wedding, Phillip and I do not share her joy. I find it beyond belief that you are even sitting in my house when neither of you have apologised for your actions, however I will allow the marriage, but it will be done properly."

Looking directly at my fiancé he continued: "As I can see it, you cannot have the means to pay for this wedding so I will have to step in. The arrangements will be made between me and Norma to avoid any further embarrassment on this family. During this time, Louise will move back home until you become man and wife. This is the only way you will have my blessing."

We sat there in shock, even mother looked dismayed (I guessed this is not what they had discussed). Unfortunately for my father, he did not know the whole situation.

I took a deep breath and started to talk.

"Unfortunately father we have not come here for your blessing, we came here on the bequest of my mother, so your terms are not remotely agreeable. The wedding will be planned between me, my fiancé and our respective mothers. We do not require your funds as we are equipped to pay for this ourselves. In respect to me returning back home that will not be happening, you wanted me out, you have got your wish."

I stood and Mr Beautiful and my mother joined me. As we said goodbye, my mother kissed me on the cheek and smiled. I felt empowered as we walked away, happy to have got out alive.

PART 4

Chapter 49

It was a Saturday morning in early March and Phillip was sitting alone at his Formica kitchen table looking at the envelope containing his divorce papers, the bright spring light was pushing against the curtains but he would not be opening them. As he looked around his empty kitchen, he wondered how he could have been so stupid, he had a beautiful wife who loved him completely but he pushed her away, now all he had left was a semi-detached house filled with memories and the smell of fish and chip packets. Sharon had left nothing behind, her silk dresses had gone from the wardrobe, the bathroom no longer smelt of Chanel No. 5, and her trademark red lipstick was gone off the hall table. The only comfort left was the bottle of brandy on the kitchen worktop, but now even that was empty and no amount of shaking would get it to release more. His father had stopped talking to him, and work had become unbearable, as his colleagues constantly gossiped behind his back. Ever since Monday morning when the heavy envelope had dropped onto his hall floor, disturbing his breakfast, he knew there was no turning back. Every morning since then he had shuddered every time he heard the postman walk up his drive, today was no different. As soon as he'd heard the light tap of a package falling onto his wooden floor he'd had a bad feeling, but reluctantly he got up to see what it was. The ivory envelope was small and good quality with elegant calligraphy on the front. He recognised it instantly, and he wanted to open it less than the heavy package waiting in the kitchen. After an hour of staring at them both he opened the small envelope first.

Mrs Norma Fraser Invites you to the Marriage of her Daughter
Louise Helena
To
Mr David Patrick Wilcox
On June 25th 1978
At St. Bartholomew's Church, Penn
Ceremony to commence at 1 pm
followed by Reception at The Connaught Hotel, Wolverhampton

It was now official, this was rock bottom.

Chapter 50

Mrs Windsor and I were sitting nervously in Mrs Hilton's formal living room. The room was overwhelmingly opulent, with thick cream carpet and heavy, pink velvet curtains. The square, uncomfortable furniture framed a large marble fireplace that was filled with a spray of brightly coloured dried flowers, even Mrs Windsor felt out of place here.

Ursula Hilton was married to Goodyear's chief executive, Patrick Hilton, she was the 'IT' woman of the county and had more formal engagements in a month than some of our other clients had in a year. If we could dress her well for one occasion, we would never have to worry about going out of business. We had been let into her mock Georgian mini mansion by the maid; we'd declined a drink for fear of spilling something onto her immaculate carpet and after a nail biting twenty minutes, Mrs Hilton strode into her decadent room and perched on the hard end of one of her settees. She was a beautiful middle aged woman with an athletic build and chocolate brown hair. Dressed head to toe in a pale blue Chanel trouser suit, cream ruffled blouse and grey courts, she made me even more nervous.

After she made a small introduction about herself, it was time for us to start our pitch. As per her request, I had prepared a sample evening dress for her to wear at a charity function on April the first, so I un-zipped the long suit bag to reveal the red silk peering from inside. Mrs Windsor explained my design as I carefully hung it onto the pre-placed clothes rail.

"As you can see, Louise has created a dress with high necked round collar, full cuffed sleeves, belted waist and A-line pleated skirt. In sharp contrast, she has cut the back into a deep V from the shoulders down to the waist, but instead of a small train she has opted for the more fashionable layered material on the skirt."

Mrs Hilton was silent and emotionless as she scrutinised the dress, and after what seemed like a lifetime she asked us to sit down.

"I love the design and the fabric" She said suddenly, her face breaking into a smile. "My only slight concern is that the back may gape, could I try it on?"

As Mrs Windsor and I relaxed our bodies in relief, we left the room together.

One hour later we were back in the car, silent in disbelief of what we had just done. Not only had the back not gaped, but the dress had fitted perfectly so after writing us a cheque for the sum of £300 she had asked Mrs Windsor to go back a week later to discuss more of her up-coming events. We were on cloud nine; this really was the boost we needed to get us to the next level.

One month after Mrs Hilton had worn our design to the April Fools Ball, our business had erupted. We had moved the centre of operations into Mrs Windsor's spare room, but I was working at least twelve hours a day, and even had an assistant. Most nights David would join me so we could go through wedding plans at the same time, but I could tell he wasn't happy about my new found fame. The more honeymoon brochures he pushed at me, the more ended up buried under waste material patches, until he just stopped talking about it. I knew that having a successful working wife wasn't part of his plan, but I was having the time of my life and I wasn't ready to give that up yet.

Chapter 51

I was lying in my borrowed bed one Sunday morning in early May, the birds were happily chirping outside and I could feel the warm sun beating against my bed, this was the first day off I'd had in weeks and I was planning on savouring every minute of it. I had been promising David a day together with no distractions and I couldn't wait to finally come through for him. As I sank deeper into the soft pillow, I cleared my head of fabric patterns and thought of the enticing holiday brochures that littered my workspace floor, then for the first time in a long time Mr Beautiful entered my mind yet again.

In my mind's eye I could clearly see David standing in the surf of my fictional beach. He was shirtless and glistening as he beckoned me to join him, before I knew it, we were dancing in the cool water holding each other close, sweat dripping down our bodies. As we swayed to a stop, he gently took me into his arms and lowered me to the sandy floor. Refreshing water rippled around my body as he pressed himself hard against me and began lightly kissing my cheeks and neck, my head sank into the soft, warm sand and I could feel myself tensing up in anticipation. As the kissing intensified yet again, I could feel the familiar storm building inside me, I pushed down hard into the fictional sand as his hand moved down my hips and into the space between my thighs, wishing for the sweet release of an orgasm ...

Unfortunately the doorbell ringing rudely awoke me from my X-rated day dream, and started an un-welcome chain of events.

Rose shouted my name, and I sluggishly pulled myself off the comforting sheets and threw on my dressing gown, then dragged my tired body down the stairs, the brightly lit hallway was empty but I followed the voices down to the lounge. As I scanned the room I saw David slowly sipping his cup of tea, Rose looking angry, and the elephant in the room was my mother sitting in the corner looking uncomfortable. As I stood just inside the small space, my glare was focused only on my mother.

"What's wrong?" I asked wearily, not really wanting the answer.

"I've been up all night, worrying about, flowers …" my mother responded.

"Flowers? You've been worrying all night about flowers? This is my first day off in months … what about the flowers?"

My mother was looking at me like a child who had lost her dummy. I couldn't believe this was how our 'perfect' Sunday was beginning.

"I'm just not happy about the arrangements in the church; I think they should be bigger." She said in anger.

"I can't believe you have stressed all night about this, why didn't you just ring us? Or better yet, just make them bigger, it doesn't bother us." I snapped back.

It was then that she started crying. This was not like my mother; I immediately put my guard back down and sat next to her.

"Is this really about flowers?" I asked concerned.

After an uneasy pause, she finally told the truth.

"Your father has left, and is living with your brother, I don't even know if he's coming back."

I was utterly shocked at this revelation, I knew my father was a tyrant but I always thought he loved my mother a little. The tears were flooding out of her and I was powerless to stop them, my heart was breaking as I sat there and watched her whole world fall apart.

Chapter 52

I had always been taught that you should keep your emotions at bay, showing them is a sign of weakness and vulnerability and therefore the things that happen to you will hurt you more. In all the time I had known my mother, she had never broken my father's rule, appearing distant and emotionless even in times of great physical and emotional pain. Today the person sitting next to me was a stranger; I did not recognise her swollen red eyes, her cracked sore lips or her greasy, un-tamed hair that she had been racking her fingers through for the past hour. All the things my father had forced her to become, he had ripped away and left her feeling lonely, lost and confused. The cynical part of me that had developed since being left with nothing was quietly pleased that she know knew how it felt, but the mother-daughter bond that somehow remained between us wanted her pain to go away, and for her to be happy.

Rose had left the house to give us some much needed space and David was standing in the kitchen, clearly upset as he stared out of the window. I had left my mother alone for a few minutes as I could feel my emotions starting to reach their climax (the last thing we needed was two hysterical women). As I stood in the hallway, I looked over at my fiancé, the very thought that a husband could turn against his wife in such a way was making me wary of the commitment I was about to make, but then my father was no ordinary husband. When I walked back in, my mother had stopped crying and was now sitting completely still, staring into the electric fire. She seemed so hollow, miles away from the woman who had proudly stood in my room on my eighteenth birthday after getting one over on my father, at this point I don't think she even remembered that day. I could see her heart was broken and that only something radical would fix it, but did I have the strength to be her rescuer like she had once been mine?

A few minutes later, David and I came up with a radical plan and before I knew it, I was alone in someone else's house, while my fiancé left to save my parents' marriage. I stood in the doorway staring at my mother, wondering what she had done to deserve all this heartbreak. Is this what loving someone uncontrollably does to you? Would this happen to me? Was I setting myself up for the biggest mistake of my life?

Chapter 53

David or Davy boy as he was known to his friends was sitting in the car outside his future brother-in-law's house, the curtains were drawn and the front lawn looked a mess. To say he was anxious was an understatement; he could feel a strong sense of déjà vu, remembering the countless times he had felt anxious before seeing Louise. He wondered how he had got to this point, how had the pretty girl on the steps of Beatties managed to turn his life so completely upside down? Suddenly he missed his old life; he missed being Davy boy, the lad who didn't want a relationship, he just wanted to have fun. At twenty three was he ready for this? Was he ready to save another one of the Fraser women?

Davy Boy stood on the front door step of Phillip's house, his pulse racing. Taking a deep breath he knocked firmly on the door and waited. As the footsteps got closer he pushed his anxieties away and took another deep intake of air. The unshaven man that appeared at the door took him by surprise; he was having trouble standing up and couldn't hold eye contact with him.

"What do you want?" the unsteady man asked him.

"I've come to talk to Michael."

"Well he doesn't want to speak to you, so you can just fuck off."

Davy Boy didn't take kindly to being sworn at, so he pushed Louise's piece of shit brother out of the way and walked down the magnolia hallway toward the dimly lit kitchen. Michael was sitting on the banquet seating inside the dining nook, hugging a half drunk Bell's whiskey bottle. In the dim kitchen he could tell that his fiancé's loser father was unshaven and wearing a wrinkled suit, Davy Boy turned on the main strip light and Michael immediately squinted up at him.

"What are you doing here?" he spat out, along with some whiskey soaked saliva.

"I've come to take you home, back to your wife." Davy Boy said firmly.

"I'm not going back to that bitch! My son was right not to have a wife and family, why would you want to be tied down by a needy woman and disappointing children anyway? I'm better off here, where I can be myself."

Davy Boy was seething, "how dare you call Louise disappointing, she has more talent and drive in her little finger than you have in your whole body" David shouted down at the pitiful man in front of him. He wondered how he could have become so bitter when he had such loyal support from his wife. It made him be so thankful for what he had at home, despite not having a father for many years now, he couldn't have asked for anymore from his mother.

Both the women in his life were at the front of his mind as he grabbed the whiskey bottle out of Michael's hands and threw it towards the floor, splashing Bell's over the plastic table. Before the glass had chance to smash onto the lino, he had Michael by the shirt collar and was pulling him out from behind the whiskey covered table. Holding him steady by his un-pressed collar he drunkenly tried to fight back but Davy Boy punched him hard in the cheek, throwing him back onto the hard plastic kitchen seat.

"Listen you piece of crap! Don't ever bad mouth your family, especially after all the shit you've given them over the years. For some reason, your wife misses you (much to my surprise) so be a man and go the fuck home, or do I have to drag you there?"

Michael looked up at Davy Boy from his hunched position in the family dining area; the glaze from his eyes started to subside as reality began to set in and he dropped his head into his hands and quietly sobbed. Davy Boy slammed down a glass of water on the table and strode past Phillip who was stood paralysed in the doorway, that mess was for Michael to sort out, not him.

Chapter 54

David had been gone some time when my mother and I had to address the elephant in the room; we had never been the type of family who talked about their problems, so the thought of exposing our feelings was nerve-wracking.

"Your father has been unhappy for a long time, he spends hours and hours sitting in his chair, staring at the television, not looking or even talking to me. Everytime I try to make any sort of conversation, he turns away from me, or just turns up the television. Most nights I go to bed alone, and its hours before he comes up, if at all, but even when he does lie next to me I just wait there wanting him to touch me, even if he just wants to abuse me, I feel that lonely."

The revelation that my mother actually wanted my father to abuse her was a shock to my ears, how could she be so lonely and desperate for human contact that she actually yearned to be raped? I didn't speak but she must have known what I was thinking as colour drained from my face.

"Your brother has been drinking a lot since he received the divorce papers. He tries to hide it when he sees me but I can tell, his eyes are red with large bags under them, and his skin looks so pale and gaunt. I am worried that your father will sink down with him; he seems so vulnerable at the moment. I can't lose them, I don't know what I would do … it would kill me …"

My mother's green eyes were searching my face for a comforting reaction but there were no words I could say right now that would make her feel better, so instead I rested my forehead on hers, and we cried silently together.

Chapter 55

Davy Boy stood in the doorway looking at his beautiful fiancé, while his future mother-in-law despaired about her marriage. The more he listened, the luckier he felt to have got Louise out of that house and away from that life. As he looked over to his guest standing just behind him, he hoped he would stay quiet long enough to hear everything, Norma bearing her soul to her daughter was just what this tyrant needed. Much to Davy Boy's shock, his guest was silent as he listened to every painful word his wife said. From the rape like beatings as she lay on their once blissful marital bed, to the feelings of abandonment when he would not even touch or acknowledge her.

As Norma finished her honest account of their once loving marriage, Michael stood motionless for a few minutes before bowing his head into his hands. He knew he had nearly destroyed his family, and Davy Boy could see the guilt he was feeling as Michael's body started to drop heavily to the ground. He grabbed him by the waist and pulled his weight up until they were both at eye level.

"Do you see what you've done?" Davy Boy whispered "I wouldn't blame her if she never came home."

As Michael found his feet once again, and steadied himself against the wall, Davy Boy saw a different kind of fear cross the old man's face. He hoped that this would be enough, as Michael gently opened the door and left his mother's house.

Chapter 56

By 5pm on our 'perfect' Sunday afternoon we were both sitting on the oversized sofa staring at Songs of Praise on the TV, not saying anything. We were uncomfortable and anxious but were feeling way to emotionally drained to do anything about it. The events of today had taken their toll on everybody; even Rose was giving us some alone time.

"Do you still love me?" David suddenly asked.

His golden eyes suddenly locked on mine as my confused mind processed the question.

"Of course I do." I said, returning his look. "It's just been a mad day and I'm still trying to wrap my head around it. I can't believe that a man could do that to a woman he supposedly loves. Where did that love go?"

I was getting more agitated as I spoke to him but he didn't stop me, I wasn't aiming my rage at him but at my father, this was years of rage refusing to be filed away any longer. "I just don't understand how you can be a husband, a father and a misogynistic bastard. I think they should make you take a test before you can marry someone, to find out if you are likely to turn into an abusive rapist." I was ranting by this point and it was giving me flashbacks from that day in the library.

"I can't believe I hate him so much, I don't want him anywhere near our wedding, and I never want to see him again!"

Mr Beautiful was sitting calmly next to me as I opened another door that I'd locked shut many years before. He didn't speak, and I didn't need him to, instead he took me into his arms and we sat together for the next few hours, just enjoying being together. No doubt we had more concerns about the huge commitment we were both about to make but we didn't need any more doors opening today.

Chapter 57

Norma walked into her flock covered hallway and directly past her husband who was standing to attention in the shadows filling the angular space. She went straight to her kitchen and turned on the bright fluorescent light, poured herself a large brandy and sat at her kitchen table. As the warm liquid ran down her throat, it calmed her instantly and her mind became clear with what she must do now. Norma's empty glass sat on her melamine kitchen table as she stared straight ahead into the harsh light. She heard Michael knock lightly on the open door before he gingerly made his way into her kitchen. Standing before the woman he had once called his wife, she had never seen him so powerless and weak, but it didn't feel as satisfying as she wanted it to. As he drew his breath and started to speak she bluntly cut him off.

"I'm going to give you an ultimatum" she said clearly and without feeling.

"You have five rules to abide by for the next six months. If you break any of these rules I will disappear, for good." She paused for a moment so that her words could fully sink in.

She was now looking directly into his eyes, and it felt good, for once she was the cold emotionless one and he looked like he was going to cry. When she was satisfied he understood, she continued.

"Number 1

You will not drink, smoke or take anything that has the power to change your personality or make you lose control.

Number 2

You will go to work every morning and will be back home by 5pm every day, you will also check in twice a day by telephone.

Number 3

You will never force your wife to do anything against her will.

Number 4

You will stay away from your daughter.

Number 5

You will take your wife to bed every evening.

There is only one other instruction, you will not attend your daughter's wedding nor will you acknowledge her in any way until I say so. Louise's wedding will be faultless and full of happiness; you owe her that at least.

Do you understand?"

As Michael looked back at her, she could tell he was grateful for the second chance, but he also seemed understandably wary. However despite his reticence that night Norma went to bed with her husband and he held her like he did the first night they were married.

Chapter 58

Rose was standing inside the indoor market, going about her business as usual when the sound of Norma's name being mentioned snapped her out of her daze. She immediately turned around hoping to see the woman who she would soon be related to, but instead all she saw were three women gossiping loudly, right in the middle of the bustling market hall. She looked these women up and down (something that had become rather a habit) and made her assumptions, all overweight, all wearing clothes they couldn't afford, all with their noses so far up in the air there should be snow on them. Rose continued to listen for the next few minutes while she queued for her sausages, but was becoming increasingly alarmed by what she heard.

Uptight Bitch in pink: "You know she kicked out her own daughter, I think it was because she did drugs, you know it's always the quiet ones. Apparently something to do with smoking marijuana at a party years ago, and she dragged that poor Angela down with her. I knew all those airs and graces she had were a front. Nobody's life can be that perfect."

Uptight Bitch in blue: "I heard that her husband left her because she couldn't control the daughter, and now she just lives in that house, drinking all day, that's why we haven't seen her in weeks."

Uptight Bitch in yellow: "I heard that the daughter's sleeping and living with a man on the other side of town, unmarried obviously, and that Norma has completely disowned her. I don't blame her really but you know if there's something wrong with the mother, there's bound to be something wrong with the daughter. It's her poor husband I feel sorry for, apparently he's had to live with his son."

Rose could feel the vein on her forehead starting to throb as she listened to these insane rumours, eventually she couldn't take it anymore and strode over to what her son would call the three 'mother hens'.

"I couldn't help but overhear what you were saying" she started to say "but you should know that I know the Fraser family personally and everything you have just said is completely untrue."

The three mother hens stood staring down at her but she was not the kind of person to be easily intimidated, so she continued.

"Norma is a wonderful woman who has been to hell and back in the last few months, as has her daughter. I am not in a position to tell you what really went on, but I can assure you the reality is much more than your stuck up minds can handle. As far as Louise sleeping and living with a man is concerned, the man in question happens to be my son, and although she may be living with us temporarily, I can assure you there are no mixed sleeping arrangements. So, as far as your completely fabricated gossip goes, I suggest you keep it to yourselves, unless you would like me to tell your husbands what you spend your mornings doing, instead of ironing their shirts."

Rose was staring at all the bitches as she watched their mouths drop and gasp in unison. "Have a nice day ladies" she said sarcastically as she walked back to the counter for her sausages, allowing herself a little smile.

Chapter 59

As rose left the market that morning, she was still feeling elated from her moral victory over the trio of bitches, it was only then that she started to worry, what if her warning had come too late? What if the gossip mill was already in full swing? She had to warn Norma, she would never forgive herself if she let the woman hear what she just had, so she boarded the bus and travelled the few stops to Maple Crescent.

As she dismounted the old red bus she could see what a pretty street it really was, the last time she was here it had completely passed her by. The short street curved around to the left and was lined with tall trees, bowing with pale pink blossoms that had started to coat the ground with their delicate pink confetti. All of the Victorian semi-detached houses had beautifully manicured front lawns that shone a deep green in the bright sunlight, it made her jealous, all she could see as she walked down her street were uninspiring semi-detached houses and driveways covered with old cars. As she approached Norma's house, she noticed that there was no car in the drive (hopefully Michael was at work, she didn't fancy seeing him.) so she made her way up to the Victorian red front door. A surprised Norma greeted her from the dark green mat and happily welcomed her in, she seemed so much happier and relaxed than any of the other occasions they had met and Rose was glad she had come.

The house was different than before, as Norma led her thorough the angular hallway, the dark smock wallpaper had been covered with family photos, including ones of Norma and Louise playing together, this made Rose smile and she now felt like she was walking through a real family home. As they walked into the living room, at the back, she noticed even more photos plus a coffee table covered with thank you letters from family members excited about the up-coming wedding.

"Would you like a cup of tea?" Norma asked, and Rose gladly accepted while she sat in the large setee that was now covered with a soft throw, making it a lot more comfortable than the last time.

"I'm sorry to disturb you like this" Rose said, as Norma placed their two mugs of tea onto the edge of the table. "It's no problem" Norma said, in a much more jovial manner than the last time Rose had dropped by.

"What can I do for you?"

Rose took a deep breath and nervously answered her friend.

"I was at the market today and I heard some women gossiping about you." She paused to allow this initial statement to sink in; when she was satisfied she carried on. "They were saying that YOU had kicked Louise out, and that it was because she had done drugs at a party a few years ago, and that you were drinking because your husband had left you. There were a few other things but I think you get the picture." Rose couldn't tell if her friend was upset or just in shock when she started shaking her head. "I thought it would sound better coming from me, rather than you hearing it on the street." Rose's body was tensed in anticipation of what was coming next and it was right to be. Almost immediately, Norma hit the roof, the quiet, reserved woman she had once known was gone and had been replaced by a tidal wave of fury.

"Who was it?" she spat out in Rose's direction "hang on I bet there were three of them, weren't there?" Rose nodded her head in agreement, not wanting to be hit by the wave. "Bitches! I knew something wasn't right, wherever I've been lately, I could hear people talking in hushed tones behind my back. I just can't believe that after years of friendship they think I'm the bad guy here, if only they knew the truth, then they'd know what it feels like to be embarrassed!"

Norma was pacing the room and breathing heavily as she let out years of frustration in one go.

"And what's this about drugs, Louise has never done drugs, I can't believe the rubbish they come out with. Did they say anything else? I need to know."

Rose sat there considering her words carefully, she had been in a situation like this before with her late husband, when he had 'needed' to know something but then had regretted hearing it. What she said next was as nice as it could be.

"They also said that Louise is living and sleeping with a man, unmarried because you have disowned her, they added that the reason Louise has turned out badly is because the daughter always ends up like the mother."

The minute the idle gossip left Rose's mouth, she felt sick, her friend had now stopped pacing and was perched on the end of her setee, staring at the floor. She was already feeling the familiar regret that she had done years ago, but she couldn't un-say it. All she could do now was wait for her to start talking, thankfully that didn't take long.

"Do you think I'm a bad mother?" Norma asked, clearly dreading the answer.

"No I don't, I think that you've had a very difficult life and have just trusted the wrong people. That doesn't mean you don't care for Louise, it just means you had hope that one day it would better. After all, in these times isn't that all we can do for our children, give them hope?"

"I still feel guilty, I wish I'd have been stronger for her, stood up for her more." Norma said as tears filled her eyes.

"We've all done things that we regret, but you haven't lost Louise, she's still your daughter and especially now that she's getting married, she'll need you even more. Just because she doesn't live here anymore doesn't mean that she doesn't need you, all that's changed is her reasons for needing you."

Rose watched as her honest words put a much needed smile on Norma's face, and stopped the steady stream of tears from falling. She knew that no amount of gossip could de-rail all the progress Norma had made in the last few weeks, and this was proof that the strong, determined woman was still inside.

Chapter 60

Norma stood at her favourite fruit and veg stall in Wolverhampton market waiting to pay for her tomatoes. June was shaping up to be a very good month, not only was her wonderful daughter getting married in three weeks but her home life had improved considerably, her and Michael had even started making love again. The spring was back in her step, and the distant memory of being the subject of idle gossip now just made her laugh. Despite this, as she placed the bright red tomatoes into her new woven shopping bag, she couldn't help but hear some of the familiar hushed voices behind her, not letting anything get her down on this beautiful bright sunny day, she decided to approach the five women who were gathered around the doorway. She recognised every person, and had once been one of them 'how desperate' she thought to herself. The hushed voices came to an inevitable stop as she wormed her way in, and stood amongst them as she once had, waiting for her opportunity to speak.

"I'm not disturbing you, am I ladies?" she asked in her new confident tone.

No reply came so she continued.

"I was wondering if you'd heard the new rumour about me, I can fill you in if you want?"

She watched intently as every woman tried to avoid eye contact with her, some even started to back away.

"What's the matter? Don't you want to be seen with the likes of me? Does lying about someone to their face not feel as good as doing it behind their back? I am sorry to ruin your fun, anyway must be off, I've got a wedding to plan. Bye!"

Norma kept her head held high as she walked through the gaggle of women, and off into the sunlit town, she still couldn't believe she had once classed them as friends, she must have felt that desperate to be part of something. Not anymore though, now she had her family back.

Chapter 61

Amy of number 36 sat behind her teller's window at Lloyd's bank, wrangling with the itchy green polyester scarf that was knotted around her neck and scratching at the layers of hairspray that held her bun together, she was tired today and not even her well fitted green skirt suit could make her feel attractive. One of her clients last night had refused to go, wanting a little bit more for his money. Eventually she had got him out, but not until 2am. By the time she had showered and tidied up, her aching body hadn't hit her small single bed until 3am. Four hours sleep wasn't contusive for a job calculating people's money and smiling, but she hoped tonight would have no surprises, just as she'd hoped that last night.

At 4.30 the bank got busy again as people came in with the days takings. Amy's head was spinning as she stamped an endless amount of paying in books and cheques. She hadn't looked a customer in the eye for 10 minutes when, the voice the other side of the glass sounded familiar. The sound was comforting to her, and made her feel safe; curious she looked up and found herself gazing into his eyes. Phillip stood before her, just as she remembered him, tall and slim (if slightly wobbly) except this time he looked sad. His face was pale and tired, and he looked as though he hadn't slept properly in months. He smiled from outside her cage, and she felt instantly energised. There was no-one standing behind him so he chatted a little; she thought he was flirting so she returned the compliment. After a few minutes of well-placed giggles and minor scarf twirling he finally asked her out for a coffee. Having instantly lost her fatigue at the sight of an attractive man she agreed to meet him later. She smiled to herself as she slowly watched the colour come back into his face, then he slowly walked away, turning back to see her of course.

Chapter 62

A newly up-beat Phillip waited patiently in Beatties top floor restaurant. The view of Victorian buildings and bustling shops out of the large windows always calmed him down; it was one of his favourite places in the town, even though he had never brought Sharon here. The cream coloured walls were filled with pictures of 'old' Wolverhampton that rattled everytime the sweet trolley was laboriously pushed passed them, along the thick blue and gold carpet. As he sat there alone, nervously awaiting his companion, he listened to the fifty or so people enjoying a late afternoon treat, swilled down with endless cups of tea. Cups and teaspoons clinked all around him while dessert forks were dragged along china plates gathering up the last tasty morsels of cake. Nearby, a group of young mothers sat near him oohing and ahhhhing as the sweet trolley, full of brightly coloured cakes and pastries was stopped next to their table, and he noticed them happily ignoring their newborn children as they chose between strawberry tarts and chocolate eclairs. He remembered coming here with his mother many years ago, she would sit opposite him looking flawlessly dressed in whatever colour best suited the season, he only ever remembered it being cerise pink, and she would delicately pour them tea, adding two sugar cubes to hers and stirring in a smooth clockwise motion. He shuddered to think that he had watched his wonderful mother become so down trodden and he longed to sit here and drink tea with her again, back to a time before he had made so many mistakes.

He had become so lost in his memories that he hadn't even seen Amy walk in. As he looked up, he saw her walking over with the blonde hostess, even in her work cloths she looked good, her long hair was pulled back into a tight bun at the back of her head and her forest green suit hugged her every curve, she looked taller than he remembered but her black court shoes were a lot higher than her furry slip-ons. As she manoeuvred her petite frame around the tables and chairs, he thought back to the time when she had given him her business card at the bank. At first he had been disgusted by it, but as the flirtation had grown stronger between them he had reconsidered. That night, all those months ago had felt wrong, despite his feelings for his now ex-wife he shouldn't have done that, as she smiled broadly at him, he hoped that he could look past their indiscretions and rescue this woman, after all he wasn't perfect either. He stood to greet Amy and pulled out her seat as she began to sit down, she hadn't taken her brown eyes off him and he had to fight the excited feeling that was building inside him. As he took his seat opposite her, he realised he had no idea what to say, this type of situation was alien to both of them and the fact that she had seen him naked was not making it any easier. For the first time in his life, he felt truly vulnerable and out of his depth, as she began to fiddle with her napkin (no doubt through boredom) he started to wonder; had he made a huge mistake?

Phillip watched as the prettiest girl he had ever seen waited for him to make his move. The tea room's vibrant buzz was starting to calm down as people with full bellies slowly made their way to the exit. The excited scraping of plates and stirring of tea had been replaced with the empty sound of money rustling and clinking on the metal thank you trays, and chairs being dragged along the heavy carpet. He was still sitting there, except now Amy was stirring her black tea to keep herself entertained. Not willing to let this be the worst date she had ever had, Phillip took a deep breath and for the first time he could remember spoke from the heart.

"I'm sorry but this is an unusual situation for me, I don't know where to start."

Amy's eyes finally met his and she seemed to relax. "Don't worry, it's weird for me too, I've never dated a … er … a 'client' before. I hope you don't find that offensive, but I don't know what else to call you."

Phillip watched as her eyes left his and she became nervous, he did feel slightly offended but she was right, he had been a 'client', what else was he supposed to be? He decided at that moment to make a decision, did he want to date this girl? Or was he willing to let another great girl go because he couldn't move on? His mind was made up the minute he saw her stirring her tea, clockwise, just like his mother. Maybe it was a slim reason but it was all he needed right now. He stood up from the table and watched her panicked eyes dart from side to side as he held out his right hand.

"Hello, I'm Phillip; it's nice to meet you."

Chapter 63

It was ten days before I was due to walk down the aisle, and the magnitude of my decision was weighing heavy on my shoulders. David had been working three shifts for six months now and was hardly ever home. The reality of what my life would be if I did give up work was scaring me, the afternoons and nights were the worst, I worked all day but by the time I got home he was gone for a long ten hours. The only time we spent together was at the weekend (as long as he wasn't preparing for the night shift) or when he was on mornings, but then he was so tired from getting up at 5am he was in bed by nine. The only silver lining was that the money was great, and we were on the way to having a mortgage deposit. But still, the thought of being in an unfamiliar house all day, just waiting for my husband to come home was too much. I decided it was time to confront David about it, but I didn't know how.

A few days later the weekend had started and he was coming off mornings and going onto afternoons. I took my opportunity on the Saturday afternoon when it was just the two of us in the house. The patio doors were open and David was sitting in his favourite chair watching TV as a cool breeze flowed over him. I sat down on the large sofa and tried to pull his attention away from M.A.S.H.

"Do you think we could talk for a minute?" I asked as he turned his head away from the Korean War operating tables.

"Of course future wife, what can I help you with?" he said happily.

"We need to talk about my job, and how you want me to give it up. I don't understand why it's so important to you."

"Oh, that" he said seemingly shocked by my question. "I thought working would be difficult for you with the children to look after."

"What children? We don't have any children, I'm only twenty!"

"But as soon as we're married we'll be trying, won't we?"

I was in shock at the outdated outlook he seemed to have, we hadn't even had sex for the first time yet and he already wanted children!

"I'm not ready for children yet, I've only just got my own life sorted out, and I'm not ready to bring another life into the world. Why would you assume this without even talking to me? Is my career not important to you?"

"Of course it's important to me, but I thought this was what all women wanted, it was good enough for both our mothers, why isn't it good enough for you?"

"I don't want to become my mother or your mother for that matter, it isn't the fifties anymore and I want more from life. I don't think that's a bad thing, when we do have children I want them to be proud of me and see me as more than their mother."

"Are you saying I shouldn't be proud of my mother, just because she doesn't work? Her life had been hard enough without having to go to work as well, and since you mentioned it so has your mother's. Are you saying you're not proud of Norma?"

I sat there stunned as I watched his face turn an angry shade of red.

"Of course I'm proud of her; I just don't think I should be guilted into living a life I don't want."

I was just as angry as him now, so I started to get up.

"I guess we're done then?" he snapped in my general direction.

Wondering where this attitude had suddenly come from I quickly snapped back.

"I can't talk to you when you're like this, I'm going to my mother's, we both need time to cool off."

I walked out of the suddenly cold living room and out of the front door, shaking my head as I went, I couldn't believe how stuck in the past he was.

Chapter 64

I was pacing around my mother's kitchen while she tried to calm me down; the thirty agonising minutes it had taken me to get there had done nothing except fuel my anger. My milky cup of tea was sitting on the melamine table going cold as I ranted about Mr Beautiful without taking a breath. "How could he be so selfish?" I shouted at my mother as she took her seat on the other side of the table. "I love my job, and I've worked hard at it, why should I give it all up, so I can wait for hours for him to come home? He thinks it's still the 1950s and I should be under his thumb, I mean it's nearly the 80s for heaven's sake, and I want to keep my independence. I might even keep my name, just to piss him off even more!" I don't know whether it was me threatening to keep my name or swearing while I said it that really angered my mom, but either way she stood up and raised her voice at me in a way that I had never heard.

"Now listen Louise, I understand that you don't want to be treated like a second class citizen, and you want to keep your independence but he is going to be your husband and he deserves your respect. I know you love him, and you don't mean these things you're saying but nonetheless you need to realise that your life is going to change and if this is something you still want to go ahead with you may have to make sacrifices. I'm not telling you to sacrifice everything but there has to be give and take."

As my mother paused to take a breath, I felt her words hit me like a punch in the face, I had never seen her be this forceful or direct and it took me by surprise. I sat back in my chair and began sipping my cold tea as she continued in a calmer manner than before.

"Being married is different to dating; you have to be prepared to make sacrifices for each other. I don't believe that you should give up your job but I do think David has a point…it means a lot to a man to be the provider in his household, despite what decade it is. He will want to take care of you and you should feel comforted by that, not threatened."

My mother sat back down as her speech came to an end, and she took my hands in hers from across the table. "All I want is for you to be happy, but if you're not ready for this, you must say now before it's too late, I don't think I could take another divorce."

My mother's tone was now warm and nurturing, but her words were no less hard to hear. One question was bouncing around my head, refusing to be filed away, 'was I ready to get married?'

Chapter 65

I was completely oblivious to the beautiful day that was happening all around me, as I walked the five minutes from my mother's house to the bus stop. I couldn't hear the diligent husbands mowing their lawns, washing their cars or teaching their young sons to ride bikes, all I could think was, how much I didn't want to go home and face what was on the other side of Rose's pristine front door. Despite my feelings, I boarded the red double decker bus and sat at the back staring blankly out of the dirty windows. As the rickety old bus rounded its final corner, the knot in my stomach began to tighten and I felt the unwelcome feeling of 'flight' wash over me, sending a momentary feeling of calm as I wondered what it would be like to just run away. When I'd left it as long as I could, I abruptly sat up from my seat and marched off the bus, as though I was going into battle. I turned the corner into the long, winding street and was greeted by the familiar sight of men's legs hanging out from under rusty old cars, and children falling off their bikes as their mother's watched from a slit in the net curtains. It felt a million miles away from the middle class street I'd grown up on, and it made me uneasy for the first time since I'd lived here.

The TV was still on, as I let myself in through the single-paned front door and down the short and narrow hallway. Bright sunshine lit up the small galley kitchen that was dead ahead of me, but I wouldn't be going in there. The second door on the right was still ajar from how I'd left it earlier and it took all of my strength to push it open. The room was still the same but the programme had changed, David was still sat in his over-sized chair with the patio door wide open, letting in a breeze that still made me feel cold, despite the warmth of the day. He didn't acknowledge me until I'd been standing there for a few minutes.

"How was your mother?" he asked in a matter-of-fact tone, not moving his stare from the programme.

"She's fine, but I think she's a bit annoyed with me" I replied.

"There's a surprise, I think I know how she feels. Does she think you're being stubborn aswell?"

"Yes, but she does see what I mean, I don't want to just be a wife and a mother, I need to be more." I wasn't thinking about the words that were coming out of my mouth, they were just automatic. "Maybe we should try and compromise, both of us get a little bit of what we want."

"So while all the other wives are cooking, cleaning and looking after their husbands, I have to deal with a woman who wants her own independence and I can just look after myself?!"

"You know that's not what I mean, and you're being very offensive. I wasn't put on this planet to serve you; just because I'm marrying you doesn't mean you have gained yourself a slave!"

By now he had joined me in the middle of the floor and we were shouting at each other, neither one of us wanting to back down.

"I'm not going to apologise for who I am, and what I've achieved, you know how hard I've worked for it, but if you are not even mature enough to listen to the compromise I'm offering then I don't think you're mature enough to get married! Maybe it's time I came to my senses and called off this wedding."

He was completely silent but his shoulders had dropped and his defensive stance had completely gone, then, for the first time since I'd walked back in, he spoke to me without malice. "What would the compromise be?"

I took a deep breath as I started to say the only words I'd pre-prepared. "I will work from home (when we have one) at least that way I will be there when you get back, but I can't give up completely, I've worked too hard."

I let my words hang in the air between us, so he could slowly absorb them, then he spoke, "So I wouldn't have to keep sitting in Mrs Windsor's spare room?"

"No, you could sit in our spare room." I replied, repeating his matter-of-fact tone.

I felt the air around him change as he got used to the idea of having a work-from-home wife, until I felt comfortable enough to approach him.

"I don't mean to sound ungrateful, because I'm not, but you of all people should know how hard I've worked to become an independent person, and how difficult it would be for me to give it up."

His golden eyes were softening as he looked deep into mine, and finally I could see the man I fell in love with. "I know how hard you've worked; I just want to look after you. I'm proud of you but it can be difficult to watch the woman you love grow to a point where she doesn't need you anymore, it can make a man feel slightly emasculated."

Suddenly I realised how childish I'd been, why couldn't I see how my success would make him feel? Especially when I'd stumbled upon it and he'd had to slog for years. I could feel my cheeks turning red and my head dropping down as my embarrassment kicked in. I hoped the patterned carpet would turn into quicksand and swallow me up. The carpet never succumbed but Mr Beautiful did, and suddenly I felt the familiar warmth from his hands around my waist, picking me back up. Looking into his eyes, I knew how much I wanted to marry him, and I felt all my fears drop away.

"So it's a no to kids straight away then?" Mr Beautiful jokingly asked as I rested my relieved head on his muscled shoulder.

"Let's have sex first, and then we'll talk." I said, as I felt him squeeze me tighter.

Chapter 66

The day before Louise's wedding, Norma was sitting on her setee having a few minutes before her daughter arrived. Her back room was warm and comforting, as the glow of the late afternoon sun filtered through her patio doors. As she sat on the soft throw that covered the functional sofa, she tried to remember her own wedding, but nothing would come into her mind. She couldn't remember her flowers, her dress or the look on her groom's face as she greeted him at the end of the aisle; it seemed years of burying any happy feelings had forced her happiest memory into hiding. There were no pictures around the house of their wedding, no mementos or keepsakes, not even a wedding present that she could use to remember the 'so-called' happiest day of her life. Things had been much different back then; people didn't give generous gifts as they do now, especially when it was a quickie wedding between two people who'd had a whirlwind romance, those things just weren't done in the country. The only thing she could remember from that time was the loneliness she felt when Michael ripped her away from her idyllic country existence, and into this bustling town. For the first few years she had really hated it, especially with a new-born son, but she had kept her head down and eventually became numb to the pain of being so far away from home. Even to this day, Wolverhampton didn't feel like home, and she longed for the simple country life that she had been ripped away from before she was done enjoying it, but Norma knew that some things would just have to remain a dream.

Chapter 67

As per tradition, I would spend the last night of my childhood in my old room while my mother slept next door. I don't know which I was more nervous about, being back in my childhood home or my impending nuptials. As I stood outside my old family home with my suitcase and wedding dress, I had vivid flashbacks of the last time I stood on this pavement, belongings in hand. Old emotions came flooding to the surface as I looked down the drive. I could see my old self shivering on the pavement with my luggage beside me, crying into the night. I decided tonight would not be a repeat of that, and I blocked the scared little girl from my mind and swallowed my tears.

The house felt different from before. My father was sleeping at my brother's tonight, so it would just be me and Mom. My mother gently prised my wedding dress from my fingers and took it upstairs while I stood in the hallway, paralysed from the waist down, clutching my suitcase like a protective shield. With all my defences on maximum, I looked around and saw that the hallway had changed, old family photos were brightening up the dark flock wallpaper and my mother's old crystal figures that I'd long forgotten about lined the sideboard, reflecting warm sunlight onto the glass covered pictures. The mood of the house had definitely changed, along with my mother, and I allowed myself to smile. Eventually, my mother persuaded me to give up my luggage and escorted me through to the living room. The room at the back of the house was bathed in an orange glow as the sun continued to set making it feel warm and relaxing, the stack of papers in the corner was gone and all the furniture had been re-arranged. An empty mug sat on a glass table, that was covered in hand-written letters and the throw on the setee was calling me to sit down. The house felt more homely than it ever had when we were a family, and it made me think. The events that had occurred, had brought us all back to where we were supposed to be.

We stayed in the living room for hours, until we were both so hungry that we had to move. In a huge break with tradition, my mother and I walked to the fish and chip shop, then consumed them out of the paper sitting on the sofa. Fish and chips were always frowned upon when I was growing up. My mother could never take the embarrassment of her house smelling like a takeaway, or being seen walking down the street carrying the tell-tale brown paper bag. After gorging ourselves on a large cod and chips each, we sat on the sofa for a further two hours, my mother listening to all my tales of working with Mrs Windsor, to how crazy men are. We never talked about all the bad things that had happened, I think we'd both talked about that enough. It definitely felt like the cloud that had been over our family had lifted, and now we could get on with our lives.

My mother had dragged herself up to bed fifteen minutes before, but I was still standing at the bottom of the stairs. The landing was dark, and I could still see the image of my father standing at the top, the whites of his eyes glaring from the darkness were an image that had been burned into my memory since that night. It had been two years since I had been up these stairs, but my feelings had not changed. My left hand gripped the bannister as I tried to lift my foot up onto the first step. As I tightened my grip and raised my right foot, I started to think of David, I still owed him from that night, when he rescued me and I hoped that over the years I would repay him. By the time I had reached the top of the stairs, my mind had filled with a new fear and had pushed the old one out. Would I be a good enough wife for him, a man that I owed my life? This new fear was flooding my mind with so much doubt that I hadn't even noticed I was standing in front of my old bedroom door. The white gloss was covered in shadows from the still moonlight that was creeping through the landing window and making shapes that would have sent a small child running into her mom's room. Luckily, I was no longer that small child and gingerly pushed the door open.

Quickly turning on the light, I could see that the room had been completely redecorated. Pale magnolia walls and new burnt orange and cream linen frightened away any monsters the moonlight had sent and made the small room feel warm and safe. As I curiously walked further inside, I saw my satin wedding dress hanging from the 1920s dark oak wardrobe that had conjured up my imagination as a child. I felt relieved to see my dress, as though I'd gone weeks, not hours without seeing it. My old fears were fading away into the night as I changed into my nightdress and slid under the crisp, clean covers, gently laying my head on the two duck feather pillowcases that I was never allowed before. As with most brides, as soon as I started to relax, my head began to fill with familiar pre-wedding nerves, until something caught my eye on the wall by the door. There, sat a small framed picture that I had forgotten existed. The black and white shot was of me being held by my mother at the familiar Wolverhampton market. I was about eighteen months old, and was wearing a little pink dress with a white bow on the back. It reminded me of a time when everything was simple. Although her marriage was already broken, just in that moment when the camera flashed, she looked so happy and content, with her baby daughter in her arms.

I pushed away the nerves until the morning and drifted off into my last single sleep.

Chapter 68

Davy Boy hated to admit it but he was drunk, admittedly, that's what you get when your best man picks you up at 4pm so you can start drinking early. It was now 10pm and walking to the bar was no longer an option, even if he could make out where the bar was, his legs definitely wouldn't carry him there. This was all Ian's fault, "You need one more night of freedom mate" he'd said, and before Davy Boy could even object, they were in his local drinking pints of 'Tenant's Super'. Unfortunately, the familiar Rose and Crown with its trusty jukebox and pool table, that was always full of people he knew, was long gone. Now they were in town and despite the gallons of beer it felt like he'd drunk, he knew where they were.

The room was filled with a yellow haze that lingered around every table, but seemed to stop just before the main stage. Purple and red lights filled the platform where once attractive women danced around poles and on chairs, dressed in nipple tassels and thongs, with only their long hair covering the rest of their bodies which only seemed perfect because of his beer tinted glasses. The Viper Room was a well known strip club in Wolverhampton, but despite its popularity he had never liked coming here. The feeling that one wrong move could get you kicked out on your backside always made him feel uneasy. David moved his bleary eyes around the cheap black bar, that no doubt was as sticky as some of the clients and he fixed his eyes on the bruiser at the bar, despite being dressed in plain clothes, he guessed that he was security. He thought he might be at least 6ft 4 but he didn't trust his instinct as he could barely see him, but his stance was giving him away, leaning against the bar with his hands clasped at his crotch, looking like he was ready to pounce.

David and Ian, along with six other blokes including 'scruffy' Steve (as Louise had nicknamed him) were sitting in a booth right in the corner of the seedy bar. The drink was no longer comforting and sociable beer, but rage inducing Bell's Whiskey, something whose affects he had come into close contact with the month before, when he had ripped it out of the hands of his future father-in-law. Whiskey was another thing he didn't enjoy, but his drunkenness was making it easier to digest. Scruffy Steve was clearly enjoying himself, as he ordered more and more women to come and shower him with twenty minutes of 'love', all his other friends seemed as happy as Davy Boy while they sat around him looking uncomfortable but especially Ian, this really wasn't his kind of thing, he preferred to be in a pub, surrounded by people he knew, not by people he had to pay to 'know'.

The more whiskey he drank, the hazier the room became, until his head hit the sticky wooden table until he couldn't take anymore, it was time to leave. As he moved his head to the right, looking for his best friend, he noticed Ian had done the same, and now they were staring at each other, presumably thinking the same thought. "We have to go" David managed in the best way his drunken lips could manage, Ian nodded his head and the two tried to help each other up. As soon as they were standing, the haze got thicker and Davy Boy felt his head spinning so he held onto a chair for support, the lights were flashing in his eyes as the two of them held each other up. They stumbled their way around small round tables where young women clad in clothes that barely covered their dignity were lurched over drunken, obscene men who were fiddling with their wedding rings, as they tried to hide their guilt. Somewhere in the distance, he heard his name but he chose to ignore it, and they carried on their way towards the exit. All of a sudden he felt his head spin out of control as he was pulled backwards onto a nearby chair. "What the fuck!" he shouted at (what he thought was) the top of his voice, but as he looked up his eyes focused on scruffy Steve standing over him, smiling right into his dazzled eyes. "It's time for your going away present mate!" Steve shouted right down his throbbing ear, his breath smelling of stale whiskey that made him heave. David moved Steve's face away from his and tried to silence his screaming head. His eyes finally focussed on the woman who was now straddling him, all he saw in the black haze that was swirling before his eyes were her big blue eyes, and bright red lips, she started to grind him then his head finally relented, falling backwards until he was no longer in control. That was the last thing he remembered.

Chapter 69

Davy Boy's eyes shot open and his swollen head filled with throbbing pain as the sound of a the neighbour's dog barking filled the quiet street with noise. All around him was dark and it took longer than he'd like to admit to realise he was lying around the toilet in the bathroom. The pale pink room was now slowing down its spin, as he dragged his broken body over to the bath and propped himself up against it. His long, aching legs were bent at the knee as he tried to fit in the small gap between the bath and the wall, but this is where they would be staying until he could figure out how they worked. Thankfully the night was still a mystery to him, as he wondered how he'd got home, unfortunately so was the fact that he was getting married today until he started to fall back to sleep. The realisation of his impending nuptials hit him like a freight train, and sent him into immediate panic. What time was it? What day was it? Had he missed his own wedding? He rolled onto his side and splashed cold water from the bath tap onto his face as he tried to calm down. Staggering onto his feet, he walked the four unsteady steps into his bedroom and fumbled around in the dark for his watch. 2am, 25th June, thank god he hadn't missed it, he fell onto his bed and was asleep by the time his head hit the pillow.

Six hours later the amnesia that had overcome him on the bathroom floor was no longer present, and the sound of his alarm, and the banging on his door sent his memory into overdrive. The image of big blue eyes and red lips was engrained in his brain, as well as the smell of stale beer and whiskey. The night before had been epic, but now he needed to wash it off him, plus he smelt like stripper and it was making him feel dirtier than ever.

He pulled himself up the still made bed that he'd slept onand propped his throbbing head against his headboard, ten seconds later his mother entered.

"Good night last night?" she asked, clearly stifling a laugh.

"I've had better" he grunted back, not able to make eye contact.

"Drink this, it'll clear your head, you've got a big day ahead of you. Oh and by the way Ian's still passed out on the floor next to the sofa, I don't think he could quite make it to the seat."

He could hear her laughing as she left his room and descended the stairs. But she was right and he smiled sarcastically at the glass of fizzing St Andrews powder that was in his hand, took a deep breath and swallowed the disgusting liquid.

Chapter 70

My head shot off the pillow before my alarm could sound, I had never been more excited than I was at that moment. I sat up in bed and looked up at the shimmer coming from my wedding dress as the early morning sunlight that fought against the curtains to be let in. Downstairs, I could hear my mother boiling the kettle with the radio on so she could happily sing along to cliff Richard 'The young ones', the whole house felt electric, and all I wanted to do was throw on my dress and walk down the aisle.

Running down the stairs while fastening my old paisley dressing gown, I could hear my mother's footsteps coming towards the hall, as soon as I saw her, I jumped into her arms and we held each other for what felt like forever. Right in that moment, I felt like that baby girl in her mother's arms, feeling so safe, protected and loved. My mother led me into the kitchen and I sat at the table where a cup of hot, sweet tea was waiting for me as soon as the hot liquid reached my throat, it calmed me down and I started to focus on what I needed to do. Suddenly, all the fears I had put to the back of my mind the night before resurfaced, OH MY GOD I WAS GETTING MARRIED TODAY!

I was so busy panicking that I hadn't noticed my mother leave the room, on realising her absence I jumped up and ran into the hallway, "Mom ... Mom ... Mom" I shouted until she came running down the stairs. "What's wrong Louise?" she asked concerned.

"I just didn't know where you were, I was panicking about today, and then you were gone and ... I ... er ... I don't know what happened."

"Louise, everyone gets pre-wedding jitters, it's normal. All you need to do is calm down, and trust me."

I wasn't being reassured by her calm voice, all I could think was how do I be a wife? What if he hates my dress? What if he's changed his mind?

Despite my mood, she calmly took my hand and led my crazy self up the stairs and into the bathroom. I could see that the bath was run, and all of my toiletries were un-packed. "Right" she said assertively "I shall leave you in peace, and don't worry all will be fine it's just a bit of bride panic." As my mother shut the bathroom door behind her, I un-dressed and lowered my quivering body into the steaming bath, the hot water instantly relaxed my muscles and, I replayed my mother's soothing words in my head as I closed my eyes and allowed myself to drift.

Chapter 71

Phillip Fraser stood looking into the full length mirror, checking his reflection as he had watched his ex-wife do a hundred times before. He really had made such a mess of things, he thought to himself, but that chapter of his life was over and now he had to move on. He had been dreading this day before the date had even been decided on and now it was finally here, his feelings still hadn't changed despite what a glorious day it was turning out to be. He could hear his father milling about downstairs but he didn't want to go down, his father had changed since mother had stood up to him and being banned from the wedding was really taking its toll. The night before, the two of them had sat in silence for over an hour, and it was only Mastermind playing on the TV that finally got him to talk. Phillip could see why he was distant but deep down he knew this was the right thing.

The phone ringing finally startled Phillip into action and he promptly answered it upstairs. A very excited Amy was on the other end, filling him in on her new outfit. He couldn't help but be proud of her, she had bought everything herself and had been happy to do so, but after all, he was paying for her flat. When they had first got together, he had made it clear that she shouldn't be living in that house, or doing her 'extra hours' (as he liked to call them), this had obviously met with financial complications so he had agreed to pay for her rent as long as she put her old house on the market, something which she did without question. He would have taken her to a registry office and married her there and then but when he did marry her, it had to be for the right reason, not simply to put a roof over her head. He had to admire her tenacity though, he had not considered how she would pay for rent until she brought it up, and he thought it was a way of making sure he wouldn't go back on his offer.

The clock read 11am when Amy finally rang off so Phillip threw on his grey jacket and finally headed downstairs. He was greeted by his father who looked happier than before.

"Very smart", Michael said with a small amount of pride in his voice.

"Thanks Dad, Mom told me to wear it, and I didn't want to look out of place."

"Your Mom always knows best, and she was right, you always did look smart in your morning dress."

Phillip could tell Michael missed his wife greatly, but he didn't want to bring it up, they didn't have the kind of relationship where feelings were discussed.

Checking his watch, he gave his dad a pat on the shoulder and headed for the door. "See you later Dad" he said as he shut the door behind him.

Chapter 72

I had spent the last hour and a half moisturising myself to within an inch of my life, painting my nails a delicate shade of pale pink, and rolling my long hair into large curlers that were sitting proudly on top of my head. As I stood looking back at the strange reflection that greeted me, I noticed how my body had changed over the years; my small boobs had gone and so had my small bum, but at least I'd stayed slim despite the other areas. As I tried to understand the woman I was now, I couldn't help but think back a few days to when I went for my first wax.

I had learned many things over the last few months, leading up to the biggest day of my life. The most painful would surely be having certain areas of my body waxed. Much to my surprise, this concept did not just apply to my legs, but to other more delicate regions of my person, apparently the modern man likes to see a neatly kept front lawn, if you know what I mean. This would be the first thing that the lady I would come to call Judas, would attempt. I was under no illusions that after twenty years of being allowed to grow free that this would be a painless process so I lay on the bed wearing just my knickers and held my breath as 'Judas' approached with the evil liquid. At first the feeling was warm and comforting, so I was lulled into a false sense of security, but seconds later all security was gone. The noise that came from ripping away years of matured foliage was not the only thing that sent a shockwave through my nether regions. I let out a high pitched wail, and was abruptly told to calm down. I instantly hated this woman, and wondered if I could avoid sex on my wedding night, so she would not have to continue. As the torture progressed to my legs, and then my eyebrows I realised that this was a reason to only get married once and the church should definitely advertise it so there would be less divorce. After a very painful sixty minutes I paid Judas and limped like John

Wayne out of the salon, feeling violated and sore. Once back, I lay down on my cool, borrowed bed and let the breeze from the open window calm me down.

Unfortunately, the waxing had been a necessary task in preparing for my bridal lingerie, which now lay on my small single bed, looking up at me. The underwear that I had been told to buy by my mother and a slightly inappropriate shop assistant, was a white lacy bra with matching French knickers that would probably spend most of my wedding day working its way up my bottom, and slowly chaffing my nipples. As I glared back at the underwear that signalled the end my virginity, I craved the days of my re-worked church dress with its buttons and ever changing hem line.

Chapter 73

Rose was standing in her bedroom liberally applying hairspray to her perm, and checking her make-up in her Grandmother's old mirror, she didn't look too bad (she thought) and hopefully everyone else would think so too. The outfit she had on was very expensive and she'd had to dip into her savings to buy it, but like Norma had said, today of all days she needed to feel good as well as look good. After putting on her dark pink lipstick she headed over to her full length mirror and gave herself a little twirl. The skirt suit she had picked was one hundred percent wool in dusky pink and felt lighter than a feather. Her knee length skirt twirled slightly at the edges, her short jacket flapped at the open buttons, and her light cream blouse became filled with warm air as she continued to spin, Rose felt like she was flying. As her spin came to an end she steadied herself on her large chest of drawers and gently lowered herself onto the bed. Thank goodness she had put on so much hairspray she thought, as she looked back at her flushed cheeks. Once her pink and brown bedroom had stopped spinning, she took a moment and looked around, how it had changed over the years. One lone wardrobe now stood where two had once occupied the space, the chair in the corner was gone and the smell of Old Spice had finally left the walls and bed linen, she couldn't complain though, she was very lucky to have had it there in the first place, but it was still something she missed deeply. Now her ancient jewellery boxes seemed to litter every spare surface, and spare bed linen took up empty space in her drawers, very little remained of the old days except something she saw everyday but today was the first day it took her attention. The old family photograph on her dressing table that was nestling behind a box of tissues and pots of face and hand creams was of the three of them, David was only five when the photo was taken and they looked so happy standing on Brighton Pier. She remembered the day as if it were yesterday, they had saved for months so that they could have a few days holiday and it had been worth every re-worked dinner and overlooked birthday. The weather was much like it was today, warm and beautiful with a clear blue sky. Patrick had held David on his lap as they rode the carousel, and she had comforted him when he felt sick from all the ice cream. They had eaten fish and chips on the beach while they dodged low flying seagulls, and walked the long promenade hand in hand as the day turned to dusk. The image of Patrick holding David in his arms as he slept, was one that she would always cherish. It was that image the doctor had told her to keep in her head ten years ago when her world slowly ended. She wished Patrick was here today to see his son get married, he would have been so proud. But more than that she needed him to hold her hand and help her through it. As she brought herself back to reality, Rose gently dabbed the small tear that had made its way down her made-up cheek and smiled to herself, today was the first time in ten years that she'd felt him here with her and her body filled with a warmth that she'd long forgotten. She got up from their bed, put on her massive pink hat and then walked down the stairs to her son, who was waiting at the front door.

"Wow mom, you look beautiful."

"Thank you Son, now let's show those rich people how it's done" Rose said to her handsome boy and his slightly hung-over best man as they walked into the waiting Rolls Royce.

Chapter 74

I couldn't take the smile off my face as my mother gently un-hooked my wedding dress and laid it down for me to step into. The heavy satin train filled the floor of my small room while I steadied myself on the old wardrobe, and gingerly stepped into my one of a kind ivory gown. I felt butterflies fill my stomach as my mother worked the fitted dress up my grown-up body as I slowly moved my arms into the straps. The dress I had been working on for six months looked different on me today as it slowly took shape while she did up the last of the zip, it suddenly looked a lot more grown up and womanly than I remembered, as it graciously gripped each of my curves. I stood silently in the mirror as my mother began to un-do the curlers on top of my head, watching as long curls bounced off my shoulders and down my chest eventually coming to rest down my back and in the deep V that made up the front of my dress. The room was all a blur when I felt her take my hair and grip the front strands at the back of my head with her mother's old hair clip, then gently run the rest through with her fingers. The smell of the strong hair lacquer brought me out of my trance and I was shocked by my new reflection. I had never felt less like a little girl, my Chanel make-up and soft hair glowed in the warm sun that was flowing through me, slowly settling my nerves and allowing me to take a deep breath for only the second time today. Before I slipped on my ivory court shoes, I turned to face my mother, she was taller than me (especially with her wedding shoes on) and at that moment she looked like an angel smiling down at me, she gently took me into her arms and we hugged for what seemed like an eternity.

The sound of the doorbell ringing woke us from our trance, and my mother made her way downstairs. I put on my shoes and a bit more lipstick, then suddenly I realised I was alone. My heart started beating quickly and I could feel the butterflies in my stomach making their way to my throat. I moved to my small window and took a few needed gulps of air as I looked out onto my family's immaculate garden, steadying myself on my old bed. In the distance, I heard my mom's footsteps coming up the stairs, so taking one last look from my old window onto the winding garden path, bright green lawn and shimmering roses, I took another breath and closed the window, just as I heard the last knock on my door. This was it, time to get married.

Chapter 75

David Wilcox was standing at the altar of St Bartholomew's Church in front of one hundred and twenty of his and Louise's friends and family. Dressed in a three piece navy blue suit he felt good, but nothing had prepared him for the nerves of having to stand up in front of all these people. The St Andrews in his system was mixing with his spiking adrenaline and he felt like he could pop. Despite his better judgement, he had invited all his mates and they took up most of rows three to five on the right of the church. Scruffy Steve had already started goading him but luckily had been knocked back down to earth by the rest of the gang. He felt like he was playing football on the Wolves pitch and everyone was watching only him, it was an intimidating feeling. In a way to calm himself, he looked over at his mother in the front row sitting happily with his grandmother, she looked happier than he could remember and had a very contented air about her. He wondered how she would cope when he moved out and her mother moved in, she did always like things a certain way and he hoped that his grandmother would respect that.

Continuing his nervous scan around the room, he saw his future brother-in-law sat three rows back on the opposite side surrounded by a gaggle of Louise's other excited family members. Despite the animation of the surroundings, he clearly wasn't enjoying himself (not being the centre of attention clearly angered him) but his date seemed happy, for some reason she looked familiar but he couldn't think from where.

David glanced at his watch and saw it had just turned twelve, somehow in all his panic he had lost the last thirty minutes. He looked to Ian, for one last bit of support and turned to face the vicar. Thirty seconds later the congregation were asked to stand.

Chapter 76

The small foyer was shaded and cool, but the heat from the June sun coming from the open front door was warming my back through my long cathedral veil, unfortunately it wasn't enough to calm me down. I stood outside the heavy church door with my right arm linked tightly around my mother's, while gripping my pink rose bouquet. My heart was beating out of my chest and I was fighting back the tears that I could feel building in the back of my throat as we stared into the un-yielding oak. I had dreamt of this moment since I was a little girl but I was petrified, and I just wanted it to be over. My mother's face was still and calm, but I could tell she was nervous, as she had gone completely rigid. The two of us were completely quiet as we heard the familiar organ start its chorus, and we moved in closer together, as the heavy doors were opened by the two ushers on the other side, revealing the path to my future.

Mr Beautiful turned and gasped as his stunning bride entered the church, his erratic heartbeat calming with every step closer to him she took; she was bathed in a pretty pink glow coming from the sun that was bouncing off the roses in her hands, and he couldn't take his eyes off her. Louise's perfect smile was framed by her gently bouncing hair and shimmering make up; he had never seen her look so beautiful. It took him longer than he realised to notice the dress that hugged her petite frame and showed off her toned, milky skin; he had never been more in love than at this moment. The one hundred and twenty strong congregation had disappeared the moment she had walked in, along with every shadow of doubt that was left in his mind, there were no shadows here right now, no darkness of any kind.

I stood at the end of the aisle smiling at my Mr Beautiful with his eyes locked on mine. I felt my mother kiss my cheek as she handed me over to the most stunning man I had ever met and then it was just the two of us. My fears were fading away, as was the rest of the room, while I looked into his sun lit face, and while the vicar started the ceremony, I remembered the first day I looked into his golden eyes. Who would have guessed that nervous little girl in re-worked hand-me-downs would now be standing here as a woman, marrying the man of her dreams.

Chapter 77

Norma took her seat in the front pew and swallowed down the tears creeping up the back of her throat, this was a day she thought would never come, and now it was here she still couldn't quite believe it. Looking around in awe at the magnificent church, she could see pink roses and white stock hanging off the pews and erupting from huge displays around the altar, framing her beautiful daughter perfectly. The last time she had seen the flowers, they had looked much less happy, all crammed together in ugly black buckets on the concrete floor of the florist's shop, but now they were smiling and shining brightly for their captive audience. Looking over at her good friend Rose, who couldn't hide the pride on her face, she couldn't help but smile, she had been right about Louise needing her, but now she had to be prepared to play a background role in her daughter's life, as she tried to overcome the challenges of being a wife.

Norma sat mesmerised as her daughter said her vows wanting to hear every last word, as though it would be the last time she would ever hear them spoken. Louise did not stutter or falter as she spoke clearly and concisely to the man she obviously adored, capturing everyone's attention in the congregation. This had to be the proudest moment of her life, never had she allowed herself to think that her shy, timid daughter would ever be this grown up or captivating, but now she didn't have to think it, she could see it happening right in front of her eyes. When the vicar started talking again, she did another scan of the church, it was then that she saw him, the dark figure standing in the shadows at the entrance. Their eyes locked and for the first time in decades, she saw the soul of the man she married, despite her warnings she was glad he came, this was something he needed to see, and hopefully now it would truly be over.

Michael Fraser stood silently in the darkness while un-controllable, un-stoppable tears ran down his face. He knew she truly hated him and he couldn't blame her … she had turned out much better without him. He didn't know what had possessed him to treat her so badly; all he knew was that he would do anything to make it right.

As his eyes shifted to his stunning wife, he longed to be sitting next to her, holding her hand. She looked truly beautiful (the way a mother-of-the-bride should), her cream pencil skirt and fitted jacket accented her slim figure and made her look ten years younger, but he especially loved her pale pink hat, handbag and gloves that as always, were perfectly matching. As he looked deep into her green eyes that had once given him so much comfort, he wondered how he could have ever caused her so much pain, when he loved her so much.

He stood and watched his new son-in-law slip the gold wedding band onto his daughter's dainty finger and then quietly slipped away, wiping the tears from his cheeks as he went.

Chapter 78

"I now pronounce you husband and wife, you may kiss your bride!" The cheers that erupted from our massive amount of guests were a distant echo to me as my gorgeous husband lifted up my sheer white veil and looked me directly in the eyes, all I could see was him. He took me into his arms and I felt a shockwave pass through me, which continued as he pressed his lips to mine. This moment is why they call it the best day of your life, not the dress, the cake or the flowers but because of the feeling you get when your husband kisses you for the first time. Every other feeling goes away and you are left with a warmth that fills your entire body, I would have stayed in that moment forever. I held David's hand tightly and pressed myself against his side as we were led to the nave of the church to sign the register. I was still in a daze as I signed my name on the parchment paper, and happily stared at my husband's wedding ring, all I could think about was the two of us being alone, so I could finally be a wife, and settle into our life together.

As we exited the church, plumes of confetti blew over us and David pulled me close into him as he battled the way through the throng of people to our waiting Rolls Royce. As my husband slipped in next to me and shut the door, the noise from outside suddenly disappeared and we were alone again. I snuggled into his arms and closed my eyes knowing I had finally come home.

Epilogue

The honeymoon suite at The Belfry Hotel was the first hotel room I'd ever seen, but I got my first glimpse from mid-air as Mr Beautiful carried me over the threshold. When he gently rested me down onto the large four poster bed that filled one quarter of the suite the size of the room startled me. I sat up on the burgundy bedspread and looked dead ahead, down the bedroom wing and into the sitting room, that were both bathed in deep reds and creams. Floor to ceiling windows ran down the right hand side of the room and I could see the bright green golf course reflecting through them, each window was framed with the heavy damask curtains in deep red that everyone with money seemed to have and light net curtains blew gently in the breeze coming from the open French window leading onto the balcony, it truly was a beautiful room. My new husband was opening every door, taking in every inch of this opulence, seeing what wonders they would turn up, so far he had found an en-suite bathroom, and the inside of some huge mahogany wardrobes. When he had completed his tour, he wandered over to the bottle of Bollinger that was sitting happily in its ice bucket on the coffee table surrounded by two glasses, a large bowl of fruit and some expensive looking magazines, not wanting to miss a single thing in the room, he popped the bottle and poured us a glass each. I happily sipped my champagne as Mr Beautiful sat at the end of the bed smiling at me, the late afternoon sun that was bouncing off the cream three piece suite and glass covered coffee table, was bathing the whole suite in an orange glow, that in turn lit up Mr Beautiful's face, causing his golden eyes to shimmer as he gazed at me, I was in utter heaven. For the next few minutes we made casual chit chat to cover the nervousness that we were both feeling, until eventually it was time to do what I had been fantasizing about for nearly three years.

Mr Beautiful stood up and removed his suit jacket, placing it delicately on the mock Georgian chair in the corner of the bedroom wing, next his waistcoat, then his tie until, eventually it was just his trousers left. Walking gracefully over to me, he took my now empty glass out of my hand and placed it on the mahogany bedside table, I could feel myself heating up with every step he took, until he was kneeling opposite me on the huge bed, my mouth opened as his eyes met mine and heat ran through my body as if I had just swallowed a fireball. I quivered as he moved closer into me and took me into his strong arms. As anxiety left my body our lips touched, and my eyes locked shut as we tenderly embraced. I felt his hands covering every inch of my body while I wriggled and quivered, and for the first time my wedding dress was in the way. My hands moved quickly around his chest (as if they knew what they were doing), and down to his trousers, un-buttoning them and pushing them down as I kissed his soft, warm lips. Finally yielding to every emotion in my body, I fell into his chest as he un-zipped my virginal dress, exposing the white lace underwear that had been hiding underneath, he took my half naked body and threw me back onto the bed and wriggled the rest of my dress free, eventually showing all of my waxed self. I felt my eyes closing as he crawled up my body and lay his hot, firm body on top of me, while he kissed my neck, down my shoulders onto my chest. My hips moved up and down as I got hotter and more turned on while he removed my bra, throwing it carelessly onto the floor and nibbled down my pulsating chest until he reached the French knickers my mother had picked. My eyes shot open and met his as my nerves reached their limit, oh god we were about to have sex! I was screaming inside my head but he never stopped looking at me as he slowly removed the only thing that was protecting my virginity until they were gone and I was completely at his mercy.

With my eyes closed and head buried in the soft pillows, I felt the heat from his naked body hitting mine as he crawled back up me, until I felt his golden eyes looking directly into mine. Letting go of any fear I still had, I opened my clamped eyes and melted into his, as he penetrated me. Slowly and gently at first, without breaking eye contact and then more vigorously as we began to move together in one motion. My back arched as he moved deeper into me and I started to dig my heels into the cool bedding, raising my hips into his, maximising the pleasure. The explosion began in my vagina and moved down through my hips, then to my legs, as he continued to thrust, our sweating bodies rolling to a stop on the fresh linen while he held me tight in his arms as I felt the pressure blow from inside me, throwing my head back. As I let go of the little girl that had once consumed me, I couldn't contain the scream that came from my mouth as the last of the explosion left my body and I clung onto his body as I moved harder and faster with him. I could feel his heart beating quicker and quicker and quicker, until his head fell back, and his whole body tensed while he clung onto my arms and we both fell back onto the soft sheets.

We were lying side by side and breathing heavily in unison as we both stared at the ceiling, blood was rushing through my body like a tidal wave and I could feel my legs quivering but I couldn't move my head from the duvet. The artex on the ceiling was making patterns as I tried to focus on a single point, and I could feel the sweat on my body go cool as the breeze from the balcony washed over me. As my breathing began to slow, I inhaled the cool air and turned to see my husband lying naked next to me. I rested my head on his gently moving chest, as he drifted off to sleep and felt the heart I had gladly given him beating away happily, safe in the knowledge that it had been entrusted to the right person.

The author

Michelle Round is an up and coming new author. Chasing Daydreams is her debut novel. Born in 1984, she lives in Wolverhampton with her husband whom she married in 2013. Michelle has had a passion for creative writing since she was a teenager. For the first fifteen years of her career, she worked in the hospitality industry. This has given Michelle a great insight into the inner workings of how people's minds work and much inspiration for her writing. As well as writing, Michelle enjoys supporting her local football team, dancing and dining in some of the best Michelin starred restaurants in London.

novum 🕮 PUBLISHER FOR NEW AUTHORS

The publisher

Whoever stops getting better, will in time stop being good.

This is the motto of novum publishing, and our focus is on finding new manuscripts, publishing them and offering long-term support to the authors.
Our publishing house was founded in 1997, and since then it has become THE expert for new authors and has won numerous awards.

Our editorial team will peruse each manuscript within a few weeks free of charge and without obligation.

You will find more information about
novum publishing and our books on the internet:

w w w . n o v u m - p u b l i s h i n g . c o . u k

Rate this book on our website!

www.novum-publishing.co.uk